Forget Nancy Shatner?

That was a tad tough to do, considering Tux was spending twenty-four hours a day with the lady. Oh, yeah, a really rough trip, especially when she looked the way she did now.

Her jeans were snug, accentuating her shapely legs and bottom. Her blouse clung to the lush fullness of her breasts. Her hair was shiny, the wild waves fetching in their gypsy-like tumble.

Yes, Nancy Shatner was incredibly beautiful.

Forgetting Nancy Shatner was totally impossible.

So forget *forgetting*. Tux would concentrate on *remembering* that she was an assignment. Nothing more, nothing less.

Tux, Bram Blue and Gibson are unforgettable men with love as endless as the Texas sky— and just waiting for women special enough to win their hearts!

Dear Reader,

Happy Valentine's Day! This season of love is so exciting for us here at Silhouette Desire that we decided to create a special cover treatment for each of this month's love stories—just to show how much this very romantic holiday means to us.

And what a fabulous group of books we have for you! Let's start with Joan Elliott Pickart's MAN OF THE MONTH, *Texas Moon*. It's romantic and wonderful— and has a terrific hero!

The romance continues with Cindy Gerard's sensuous *A Bride for Abel Greene*, the next in her NORTHERN LIGHTS BRIDES series, and also with Elizabeth Bevarly's *Roxy and the Rich Man*, which launches her new miniseries about siblings who were separated at birth, THE FAMILY McCORMICK.

Christine Pacheco is up next with *Lovers Only*, an emotional and compelling reunion story. And Metsy Hingle's dramatic writing style shines through in her latest, *Lovechild*.

It's always a special moment when a writer reaches her **25the book milestone**—and that's just what Rita Rainville has done in the humorous and delightful Western, *City Girls Need Not Apply*.

Silhouette Desire—where you will always find the very best love stories! Enjoy them all....

Lucia Macro

Senior Editor

Please address questions and book requests to:
Silhouette Reader Service
U.S.: 3010 Walden Ave., P.O. Box 1325, Buffalo, NY 14269
Canadian: P.O. Box 609, Fort Erie, Ont. L2A 5X3

JOAN ELLIOTT PICKART

TEXAS MOON

SILHOUETTE *Desire*®

Published by Silhouette Books

America's Publisher of Contemporary Romance

SILHOUETTE BOOKS

ISBN 0-373-76051-5

TEXAS MOON

JOAN ELLIOTT PICKART

is the author of over sixty-five novels. When she isn't writing, she enjoys watching football, knitting, reading, gardening and attending craft shows on the town square. Joan has three daughters and a fantastic little grandson. Her three dogs and one cat allow her to live with them in a cozy cottage in a charming small town in the high pine country of Arizona.

For my fourth daughter, Autumn Joan Pickart.
Born June 21st, 1995—Nanjing, China.
Home September 27, 1995.
And for Hand in Hand International Adoptions,
the miracle makers.

Prologue

"**W**ell, now I declare, isn't this the nicest surprise? You've come to visit Granny Bee. Bring yourself in and have some homemade lemonade. I still make my honey, of course. Was how I got my name Granny Bee.

"Tell you a story? Land's sake, I've been spinnin' tales as far back as I can remember.

"How would you like to hear about the Bishop boys? Now then, Tux is the oldest, then a year later along came the twins, Blue and Bram. There was so much love in that big, old shabby house, you could feel it by walkin' in the door.

"Jana-John, the boys' mama, has been paintin' pictures ever since I can recall. She doesn't give a hoot if they're any good. She's happy paintin', and that's just fine.

"The boys' daddy is Abraham Lincoln Bishop, and I swear he truly does have the looks of Mr. Lincoln. Abe Bishop was a history professor 'fore he retired. Now he writes long papers on history doin's, but I've never heard tell of what he does with the things once he writes 'em.

"Now Tux, it was found, had psychic powers. He can see in his mind somethin' that's goin' on far away. He doesn't fancy doin' it, 'cause those powers are embarrassin' to him, makes him feel like folks might not accept him as the person he is, and would figure he was strange. He'd just as soon no one knew 'bout those powers.

"A while back, the boys sat 'round the table with their folks, and the brothers decided it was time to marry and have some babies. It was as good as done, they thought, as they were used to doin' what they set out to do. Well, findin' the right person to love isn't all that easy. Those boys were in for a mighty big surprise.

"Now, I told you 'bout Tux's powers, that he didn't like havin'. You can just imagine how upsetting it was when those pictures started comin' without him doin' one thing to bring 'em. Tux didn't like that one little bit.

"But, my stars, that's exactly what was happenin'...."

One

___

Tux Bishop shot bolt upright in bed, the sound of his pounding heart echoing in his ears. He took a deep, shuddering breath, then dragged both hands down his sweat-soaked face.

"Damn it," he said, then threw back the sheet and left the bed.

The clock on the nightstand glowed the message that it was just after two in the morning. As his eyes grew accustomed to the darkness, Tux began to pace naked around the large bedroom.

This was the third night in a row, he fumed. He'd been jolted awake, heart racing, dripping with sweat, three times now.

The dreams he'd been having were not dreams...at least not in the usual sense of the word. *That* fact was what had him tied in knots and mad as hell.

Tux sank onto the edge of the bed, rested his elbows on his

knees and made a steeple of his fingers, tapping it against his lips.

Slow down, calm down, he ordered himself. Ranting, raving and wearing out the carpet wasn't going to get him anywhere. He had to analyze the situation and try to determine what in the hell was going on.

Yes, okay, he had psychic powers that enabled him to glimpse events taking place anywhere in the world.

But…and that was a very big but…the only way his psychic abilities could be put into operation was by him going into deep meditation, a near-trance, that left him drained and exhausted.

He preferred not to use his detested powers, and rarely did so. He had, in fact, totally ignored them for many years.

But now?

"Damn it," he said, shaking his head.

He knew that the dreams he'd had for three nights now were not really products of his subconscious mind.

They were *not* dreams.

The images were psychic messages that had come to him unbidden.

Why?

Even more, how?

He commanded his psychic powers. Outside forces did *not* dictate when his unwelcomed ability would be activated.

Tux stretched out in the bed again, laced his hands beneath his head and glowered at the ceiling.

He had two choices. He could ignore what was happening and hope it was a short-lived fluke and had run its course. Or he could square off against it, take a close mental look at the scenes that had come to him, and attempt to sift, sort, then dismiss them once and for all.

"Yeah," he said. "No contest. I'm the one who's in charge here."

So, okay, he'd start at the beginning.

The first night he'd seen a shadowy figure with no discernible features, or a clue as to whether it was a man or woman. Swirling around the figure was a dark maze of what appeared to be beads or balls of some sort.

The second night the maze had been clearer. The dark cloud had become brightly colored beads, as well as buttons. The beads had separated into straight rows. The shadowy figure had been far from clear, but it was most definitely a woman.

Then tonight there had been even more. He'd had a glimpse of a sign that read: Buttons and Beads.

He'd also seen the woman. She had dark eyes and a wild tumble of black hair that fell to her shoulders in curly disarray. She was very lovely with a gypsylike appearance that was accentuated by a bright blue shawl she'd been wearing.

She'd been holding out her hands, as though pleading for someone to come and help her, and tears had flowed down her pale cheeks.

And on all three nights, he'd sensed the cold chill of danger.

"Lord," he said, and pulled his hands from beneath his head and dropped his arms heavily onto the bed.

He needed a plan of action. The thought of enduring a fourth night like this held no appeal. Whatever was triggering his psychic powers had to be stopped before he went nuts.

"Buttons and Beads." He rolled onto his stomach, punched the pillow, then lowered his head again with a weary sigh.

First thing in the morning, he thought, as sleep began to creep over his senses, he'd track down a place named Buttons and Beads. Even if it meant talking to every telephone information operator in the country, he'd find it.

Nancy Shatner finished counting the glossy red beads, then scooped them into a plastic bag. She slipped the bag through a slot in a small white machine that sat on the table, heat sealing the bag.

Next came a sticker with the name, address and telephone

number of the shop, which she pressed into place in the lower right-hand corner of the bag.

After checking off the red beads on an order form, she carried the rectangular hard-plastic bin to the front of the store and set it in its designated place, returning to the rear work area with a bin of blue beads.

Settled once more at the table, she checked the order form, nodded, then lifted a handful of blue beads from the bin to a large felt mat. Using what was actually a frosting spatula, she began to quickly move beads two at a time from one side of the mat to the other.

"Two, four, six, eight," she said aloud, then continued to count silently.

She made piles of twenty beads, which she would recount before sealing them into a bag.

After making five piles of twenty, she took a sip of tea from a ceramic mug, wrinkling her nose as she discovered it was cold. Setting the mug to one side, she stretched her arms above her head, then dropped her hands to her lap, smiling as her gaze fell on the stack of orders she was filling.

Business is booming, she thought. Her reputation for quick service and a product of superb quality was growing. Her mail-order catalog with *colored* photographs of the buttons and beads was worth the extra money she'd crossed her fingers and paid.

Nancy switched her gaze to the far end of the large table where she was just beginning to start the assembly of a new catalog, which would have a special sale section to mark the celebration of Buttons and Beads being officially two years old.

The walk-in trade, she mused, was increasing nicely, much to her surprised delight. The area of town where she was located wasn't exactly a high-class shopping mecca. It wasn't a high-class anything, for that matter.

The decision to set up the front area attractively for whatever retail business she might garner had been a good one. It was easy enough to tote the bins to the rear area to fill mail orders, and she considered every face-to-face sale a bonus.

"Life is a bowl of cherries," she said, then laughed. "Or whatever. Get to work, Ms. Shatner."

Over the past two years, she'd perfected the knack of being able to count with one section of her brain, and think about whatever struck her fancy with the other part of her mind.

A fact, she thought merrily, that had probably kept her from turning into a blithering idiot from spending her days counting two, four, six...

Life is a bowl of cherries? she mentally repeated, as she slid blue beads from one side of the mat to the other. Now that she really thought about it, that didn't make much sense. What if a person didn't like cherries?

The bottom line was that her life was in shipshape order. She was happy, fulfilled and contented. Her fledgling business was doing well, and she had marvelous friends in the store's shabby, run-down neighborhood. She had everything she wanted and needed.

Well...

Nancy frowned slightly as she continued to count the beads.

There were moments...not often, but once in a while... when she was a tad lonely. Sitting alone in her little apartment above the store, watching a romantic movie on her minuscule television, sometimes caused her to wistfully yearn for a special man, a wonderful man, to take her into his arms.

"Hush, Nancy," she said. "Eighteen, twenty," she added, completing a pile of beads.

She stared into space.

It was perfectly understandable, she reasoned, that she'd have fleeting thoughts of being loved and loving in return, of having a child that was a miraculous result of that love. She was, after all, a normal, healthy twenty-five-year-old woman.

But the fleeting thoughts were just that...fleeting. She valued her hard-won independence far too much to relinquish it for any reason. To enter into a relationship with a man would require her to give away a part of her being, and to be accountable to someone other than herself.

No.

Never again.

"Stop it," she scolded herself. "You'll make the bowl of cherries gloomy by thinking about that stuff."

Blanking her mind beyond counting, she began to hum a peppy tune.

Tux stood across the street, frowning as he stared at the store with the sign hung on the top front that read Buttons and Beads.

It was a typical June morning in Houston, hot and humid, but Tux was oblivious to the trickle of sweat running down his back beneath his cotton shirt.

It had been ridiculously easy to find the store with the sign he'd seen so clearly in the images in his mind. He'd simply opened the Houston telephone book to the yellow pages, and there it was.

He folded his arms over his chest and leaned one shoulder against the chipped bricks of the front of the deserted building behind him, sweeping his gaze along the street.

It was a mishmash of structures. Some, like the one he'd propped himself on, were empty, the whitewashed windows and crumbling brick walls covered in spray-painted graffiti. Others had professionally produced signs like the one announcing Buttons and Beads, sparkling clean windows and walls, and nicely painted front doors.

He could see a variety of businesses—a bakery, a used clothes store called The Second Time Around, a pawnshop, a small grocery store, and some others he couldn't quite decipher from where he stood.

The height of the buildings, combined with the curtains in

the upstairs windows of the occupied ones, indicated that the owners, or possibly other renters, lived above the stores.

There was pride of ownership there, as well as evidence of broken dreams and a failure to succeed. But the effort of sprucing up that the tenants or owners had made couldn't erase the section of the city they were in.

Dangerous.

"Damn," he muttered.

He did *not* want to cross that street and go into Buttons and Beads. There was a knot in his gut the size of a bowling ball caused by the dread of what he might find.

Tux shook his head in self-disgust.

Some former government agent now a private investigator *he* was. He was shaking in his shorts over what he might discover beyond the door of that shop. The woman he'd seen in the visions, that beautiful, gypsylike woman, had been in danger, had been pleading for help as she cried tears of fear.

His psychic powers didn't see into the future, never had. He could glimpse only what was taking place at the actual moment, or had *very* recently occurred.

Why the foggy and confusing images of what might have taken place in that store had reached him without him bidding them to come, he didn't know. Hopefully it was a fluke that would never happen again.

Maybe... Yeah, that was a comforting thought. Maybe the scenario he'd witnessed had occurred years before, and had accidentally landed in his brain.

Granted, the card on the door of Buttons and Beads said Open, but it could very well be that he'd walk in there and find a little old man running the place.

The old guy would relate a sad tale of a robbery years before that had caused the young woman, who then owned the shop, to be slightly...very slightly...harmed. She'd hightailed it out of there after recovering from *minor* injuries suffered during the assault, and was now happily married with five kids.

Tux blew out a puff of air from a pent-up breath, then told himself to cross that street.

Now.

Mumbling several earthy expletives, he pushed himself away from the wall and started slowly forward.

The brass bell above the door tinkled, alerting Nancy to the fact that someone had entered the store. She continued to count, cocking her head to listen for a greeting from a friend in the neighborhood. They all knew to call out a hello of some sort, then wait until she had finished counting the beads into a pile of twenty.

Realizing that a real customer was out front due to the absence of a familiar holler, she dropped the frosting spatula and got quickly to her feet to hurry from the rear area.

As she came through the doorway, she was smiling pleasantly.

Tux's shoulders slumped in defeat when he saw the woman who had emerged from the back of the shop.

It was her, he thought dismally, the woman from the visions. There she was, with her wild tumble of shiny black curls, big dark eyes and lovely features.

She was wearing a white peasant blouse that accentuated her slender throat, and a multicolored skirt. There *was* a gypsylike aura to her, just as he'd seen in the haunting images.

She was absolutely beautiful.

And he wished to the heavens that she wasn't standing there in front of him.

Also taunting him were the bins of beads separated by color, representing the columns he'd seen in the visions.

Tux frowned and shook his head.

"Oh...hell," he said, glaring at the woman.

Nancy blinked in surprise at the man's unconventional greeting.

Not, she admitted, that *she* had said anything cheerful or welcoming. She'd been momentarily struck dumb by the unexpected presence of one of the most gorgeous men she'd ever seen.

He was about six feet tall, had need-of-a-trim blond hair that was sun-streaked to nearly white in places, a marvelous tan, and incredible blue eyes. A pale blue dress shirt covered broad shoulders and chest, and a flat belly. His jeans were faded, the now soft material hugging narrow hips and powerful legs.

Gorgeous, she reaffirmed in her mind.

"Oh, hell?" she repeated, moving to stand behind the row of bins.

Still glowering, Tux closed the distance remaining to the bins.

"Do you own a bright blue shawl?" he said gruffly.

"I beg your pardon?"

"Just answer the question."

Nancy planted her hands on her hips. "I certainly will not. If you're attempting to sell shawls, you've got a lot to learn about how to approach potential customers, mister. You're rude, pure and simple. Goodbye."

Tux stared up at the ceiling for a long moment, then looked at the woman again.

"I'm sorry," he said. "Let me start over. I'm Tux Bishop."

"Nancy Shatner," she said, eyeing him warily.

"Hello, Nancy." Tux paused. "Do you own a bright blue shawl?"

"Goodbye, Mr. Bishop," she said, folding her arms beneath her breasts.

"No, no, wait," he said, raising both hands. "I'm not selling anything."

"That's good," she said dryly, "because with your oh-so-charming personality you couldn't pay the rent by being a salesman." She leaned slightly toward him. "Just what exactly is it that you want?"

Oh, lady, Tux thought, that was not a terrific question for a beautiful woman to ask a red-blooded, healthy man. With no stretch of the imagination whatsoever, he could visualize taking Nancy Shatner into his arms, nestling her to his body, then capturing her tantalizing lips with his own.

Whoa, Bishop, he ordered himself. He could feel the heat low in his body, coiling, twisting, turning. He wasn't there intent on seduction. He needed answers to what had happened to him and why it had taken place, before he went out of his ever-lovin' mind.

"Mr. Bishop?"

"What? Oh, call me Tux."

"Why?"

"Because it's more friendly, Nancy."

"It's *Ms.* Shatner. You don't evoke friendliness, not even close. Look, I'm very busy, Mr. Bishop. I don't want to be rude, but I'm rapidly approaching having no choice. Please state your reason for being here...*now*."

"It's a long story."

"I don't have a long time to listen. Give me an edited version."

This, Tux thought, was not going well. He needed to start over.

He flashed Nancy his best, hundred-watt, knock-'em-dead smile.

Good grief, Nancy thought, Tux Bishop smiling should be declared against the law. That smile probably had women dissolving into puddles at his feet. Well, not Nancy Shatner. So what if her heart had actually skipped a beat and a frisson of heat had slithered down her back? It didn't mean a thing.

"Nancy," Tux said, still smiling, "look, it's an easy enough question that won't cost you one penny to answer. Do you own a bright blue shawl?''

"No.''

"No, you won't answer the question? Or no, you don't own a blue shawl?''

Nancy sighed. "I have several shawls, but not a bright blue one. I have never owned a bright blue shawl. Does that complete your survey? Are we finished here?'' She nodded. "We're definitely finished. Goodbye, Mr. Bishop.''

"Tux. Listen, I... Oh, hell.''

"That's how this conversation started. So, oh, hell, to you, too, and goodbye.''

"Nancy,'' he began, a serious expression on his face, "I have to explain something to you. It's very important, it really is. I realize that the last thing a woman wants to hear from some fool of a guy dumb enough to say it is 'trust me,' but that's what I'm asking you to do. Trust me. Give me some time to tell you what's going on.'' He paused. "Please.''

No? Yes? Nancy thought. Darn it, he suddenly sounded, even looked, concerned, or worried, or... There was a sincere quality to his voice now, too, edged with a touch of...what? Panic? Urgency?

Trust him? Why should she? He was obviously after something, but heaven only knew what. Was the concern she was witnessing real, or was he a very practiced actor?

No, forget it. She was sending him packing right this second.

But then again, she was admittedly nosy enough to want to discover what he wanted from her.

"Well,'' she said, "all right, you may have five minutes, but you'd better make this good, Mr. Bishop.''

"Thank you, Nancy. Is there somewhere we can go and sit down?''

"No. You stay right where you are. Speak. You're using up your time.''

Tux sighed. "Yeah, okay. Try to keep an open mind, will you?"

Nancy looked directly at him, no readable expression on her face.

"You're difficult to deal with, do you know that?" Tux said.

Damn, he thought, he'd decided to jump right in and tell Nancy about his psychic powers and the visions he'd seen. As uncomfortable as he was with his so-called *gift*, he'd felt there was no other way to handle this besides just blurting it out.

But he suddenly didn't like that plan. He was standing in front of a very beautiful woman, and he had no intention of watching her narrow her eyes, take a step back, and mentally label him as strange.

He did not, however, want to lie to Nancy Shatner, either. This was going to have to be handled very carefully, with expertise, finesse.

"Hello?" Nancy prompted. "Your five minutes is ticking away very rapidly, Mr. Bishop."

"Tux." He took a deep breath and let it out slowly. "Okay, here goes. I know this guy who has psychic powers. We're very good friends, even if he is a step off from normal because he has visions, you know what I mean?"

"And?"

"Well, I humor him, because he's my buddy. Friends do that for friends." He was *not* lying to Nancy. He'd read magazine articles that said a person should be their own best friend. "Besides, my…friend's visions are usually right on the mark when he has them. Anyway, he had some visions about…about you."

Nancy blinked, opened her mouth, closed it, then tried again.

"What?" she said, more in the form of a squeak.

"It's true. He saw you, and you were wearing a bright blue shawl."

"But I don't own a blue shawl."

Tux ran one hand over the back of his neck. "So you said, and that muddies the waters even more. Damn, this doesn't make any sense."

"It's crazy, that's what it is," Nancy said. "Who is this friend of yours? Why didn't he come here himself? I don't know very many people in Houston. Why would *he* know *me?*"

"You don't have to know a person to have psychic images about them. My friend is sensitive about his powers, and doesn't like to discuss them, so that's why he sent me. The thing is, he doesn't have the ability to see into the future. He can only glimpse what is taking place at the moment, or very, *very* recently. That's why I said this *really* doesn't make sense."

"Is he certain he saw me?" she asked, leaning slightly toward him. "Absolutely positive?"

He nodded. "Yes. He saw the Buttons and Beads sign that's on the front of your store. That's how I was able to find you this morning."

"Dear heaven, this is creepy," she said, wrapping her hands around her elbows.

No joke, Tux thought dryly. Nancy was having the usual reaction to an announcement like the one he was making. It was creepy. *He* was creepy. He was glad he hadn't told her that *he* was the one with the psychic powers.

"Well," Nancy said, "what was I doing? You know, what was taking place in the visions?"

Oh, hell, Tux thought, he didn't want to scare her to death. What should he say? It wasn't as though he had any experience in predicting the future. How did he even know there was any validity to what he'd seen? This whole situation was confusing *and* very disturbing.

"Mr. Bishop?" Nancy persisted. "Tux?"

"What?" he said, snapping back to attention. "Oh, the visions that you were in. Well, it was a mishmash of things, you understand.

"The buttons and beads were swirling around as though they were being whipped by a wind, then they settled into columns, rows, which I assume were those bins you have there.

"The painted sign saying Buttons and Beads came into view, then disappeared. My friend doesn't see images like a movie, all neat and tidy and organized."

Nancy nodded. "I've got it. So? What was I doing in the mishmash?"

Tux began to search his mind frantically for what he should say. For all he knew, the visions had meant nothing because he really didn't possess the power to see into the future.

On the other hand, if by chance this once…and it better not happen again…he actually *had* glimpsed a scene of something that had not yet taken place, but *was* going to happen, Nancy deserved to be warned of the danger that she might be facing.

Then again, she didn't even own a bright blue shawl.

He was going nuts arguing with himself. He was chasing his own thoughts around in his head like a hamster in one of those endless wheels that went nowhere.

Tux cleared his throat. "Yes, well, you want to know the part you played in what my friend saw. That's certainly a reasonable request. I—"

He was interrupted by the tinkling of the bell over the door as a short, plump woman in her sixties bustled in, carrying a grocery sack. Breathing a mental sigh of relief at the reprieve, Tux stepped back out of the way.

"Hello, darling," the woman greeted Nancy. "How are you this lovely summer morning?" She glanced at Tux. "Oh, you have company. Go right ahead with what you were doing. I'll wait."

"We're just chatting," Nancy replied. "Glenna Cushman,

this is Tux Bishop. Tux, Glenna owns the used clothes store down the block.''

Tux smiled. ''It's a pleasure, ma'am. I saw your shop. The Second Time Around is a clever name.''

''I know,'' Glenna said, laughing merrily. ''I was so tickled with myself when I thought of it.'' She slid her gaze over Tux from head to toe, then back again. ''Hmmm, aren't you a dandy hunk of stuff? Yummy.'' She looked at Nancy. ''Nancy Shatner, please say you noticed that this is one very sexy man.''

Tux laughed.

Nancy blushed a pretty pink and rolled her eyes heavenward.

''Glenna, please,'' Nancy said, with a moan. ''Hush. All right?''

''Well, facts are facts, dear,'' Glenna persisted. ''The man definitely does wonderful things for a pair of jeans. Beads and buttons simply won't keep a woman warm on a snowy winter night.''

''Glenna,'' Nancy said, leaning slightly toward her, ''this is Houston, Texas. We don't have snowy winter nights.''

''Figure of speech. You know what I mean,'' Glenna said. ''You're young and beautiful. You need a man in your life. Tux, don't you think Nancy is beautiful?''

''Glenna,'' he said, his voice very low and rumbly as he looked directly at Nancy, ''I think Nancy is extremely beautiful. She reminds me of a gypsy. Oh, yes, she is definitely beautiful.'' And now he knew she was unattached, was not involved in a relationship with a man. Thank you, Glenna Cushman.

Dear heaven, Nancy thought, unable to tear her gaze from Tux's mesmerizing blue eyes. She could hardly breathe and her heart was beating like a drum.

Tux's voice had dropped an octave, and she felt as though it were caressing her like dark velvet, creating thrumming heat as it swept over and throughout her. Tux Bishop was having a very unsettling and unwelcomed effect on her, drat him.

"I must dash back to the store," Glenna announced, breaking the strange sensuous spell that had weaved around Tux and Nancy. "I just took some things that came in late yesterday out of the washer and dryer. Per usual, my darling girl, you get first pick. I thought this was perfect for you."

Glenna reached into the sack and whipped out a garment that she flipped onto the top of the bins in a splash of color.

It was a bright blue shawl.

Two

Nancy stared at the blue shawl as she agreed absently with Glenna that it was lovely. The older woman reminded Nancy once again how handsome Tux was, then hurried out the door to return to her own store.

"Tux?" Nancy said. She tore her eyes from the shawl to look at him. "You told me your friend couldn't see into the future."

"He can't." He frowned as he met her troubled gaze.

"But he did. He saw me wearing the shawl before it belonged to me, and now here it is."

"Yeah, here it is." He ran a hand over the back of his neck. "Why would he suddenly glimpse something from the future? I can't accept this."

"Oh, really?" Nancy returned, her voice rising. "Pitching a fit isn't going to change the fact that I now own a bright blue shawl. You keep dancing around the subject of what was happening to me in those visions. I want you to tell me."

Once again the tinkling bell over the door announced the entrance of someone into the store, and once again Tux sighed inwardly with relief.

An attractive, middle-aged woman, who was smartly dressed in an obviously expensive sundress with a matching wide-brimmed hat, went to the row of bins.

"Good morning," the woman said, smiling at Nancy. "I need some beads for a blouse I'm having made. It has a Western style, and I thought it would be nice if beads were added to the fringe. A friend told me about your store, so I drove all the way over here to select the beads myself."

"I appreciate your making the trip," Nancy replied pleasantly. "Now then, what color is the blouse and what kind of material is it being made from?"

Tux tuned out the discussion between the two women. He shoved his hands into the back pockets of his jeans and wandered around the narrow area making up the front portion of the store.

There was a lot of inventory in a small space, he mused. Nancy Shatner had used every inch of room to advantage. The sun pouring in the gleaming front window cascaded over the bins of buttons and beads, creating an extremely appealing kaleidoscope of color.

There were more beads than buttons, he noticed. The beads were a variety of every shape, size, color and material imaginable. There were even leather beads, as well as some that looked like delicate crystal.

Tux stopped in front of the two bins holding the buttons. He picked up a square button that appeared to be hand-painted china, then carefully replaced it. The next one he scrutinized was a replica of a buffalo nickel, the one after that a tiny wooden log.

Fascinating, he thought, and very clever. It would be interesting to know how Nancy had come to the decision to operate such an unusual business. It would, in fact, be interesting to know more about Nancy Shatner herself, the woman.

Tux went to the front window and stared at the shabby, empty building he'd leaned against across the street.

Surely Nancy didn't live above Buttons and Beads, he thought. This was definitely *not* a neighborhood for a woman alone to take up residency. Not even close. It wasn't that great a location to operate a business, but low rent had no doubt enticed Nancy to set up shop here.

Her reputation for having quality merchandise was obviously spreading, as evidenced by the arrival of Mrs. Megabucks from across town. He had to give Nancy credit for what she'd accomplished, that was for sure.

"There you are," Nancy said, handing the woman a white bag. "Thank you so much. Your blouse is going to be beautiful. I tucked one of my catalogs into that bag so you can browse at your leisure, and I'll put your name on my mailing list so you'll be notified of special sales in the future."

"Marvelous," the woman said. "I'll certainly tell all my friends about Buttons and Beads. Some won't come into this section of town, so I'll share the catalog, too. Goodbye for now."

"Goodbye," Nancy said, "and thank you again."

The woman left the store, and Tux turned from the window to look at Nancy.

"You seem to have everything covered from A to Z," he said. "I'm impressed, ma'am."

"Thank you, sir." She smiled as she dipped her head slightly. "What kind of work do *you* do?"

"I'm a private investigator," Tux said, walking slowly back toward the bins.

"Really? I've never met a detective before. Were you a police officer?"

"No, I worked for the government until about a year or so ago."

"Ah, I see. Then you were, no doubt, a secret agent of some kind."

Tux frowned. "I didn't say that."

"It's obvious. You worked for the government. If you'd been a mailman, or internal revenue clerk, or social security expert, you would have said so. Besides, secret agents who get tired of dashing all over the world are perfectly trained to become private investigators." She shrugged. "That's how it goes in the movies, and it makes sense to me."

Tux chuckled. "You're really something. You're also right. I don't announce that I was a government agent. People either start asking me questions about what they believe must have been an exciting life, or I make them nervous and they close up." He paused. "Do I make you nervous, Nancy?" He looked directly into her dark eyes.

"No," she said quietly.

Oh, Tux definitely had an unsettling effect on her, she admitted silently, but it had nothing to do with his former or present occupations. It was Tux Bishop, the man, who was throwing her off-kilter, causing funny flutters of heat to whisper throughout her. He was just so incredibly, blatantly *male*.

She lifted her chin a tad. "I believe that everyone should try to know who they are and discover what they want. Then they should move forward and go after their goal, their dreams and…"

Nancy's voice trailed off and she averted her eyes from Tux's.

"Whatever," she finished saying after a moment. "I didn't mean to get on a soapbox about it. Just erase all that. You didn't ask for a sermonette."

Tux looked at Nancy intently, suddenly wishing his powers…which were usually annoying…included the ability to peer into a person's mind. To be more precise, into Nancy Shatner's mind.

Who had tried to keep her from going after her goals, her

dreams? he wondered. Her voice had rung with determination, conviction…and, yes, passion.

"If I'm nervous about anything," Nancy said, "it's your apparent reluctance to reveal to me what I was doing in the visions your friend had and what was happening to me. Is there some reason you don't want to tell me what he saw?"

"Of course I'll tell you, Nancy," Tux said, "but I want to be certain you understand that this whole thing could be a false alarm."

"Fine. Now explain my role in the scenario that your friend saw."

"Yeah, well," Tux began slowly. "I realize I've been postponing telling you, but I didn't want to scare you. Nancy, my friend sensed danger during all three visions. When he could finally see you clearly, you had on the shawl, you were crying and holding out your arms as though pleading for help. He sensed you were frightened."

"Oh, dear," she whispered. She pressed trembling fingertips to her lips.

"I'm sorry," Tux said miserably.

On impulse he strode past the end of the bins to where Nancy stood behind them, and wrapped his arms around her.

"I'm sorry I frightened you," he repeated. "I feel so rotten about this, especially because I can't explain why or how it happened. If I…we, my friend and I…could figure it out, it might help to ease your fears."

Nancy encircled Tux's waist with her arms and rested her head on the solid wall of his chest.

Oh, he felt so good, she thought. He was strong and powerful. Yes, she was determined to be independent, to take care of herself, answer to no one but herself, but, oh, God, this whole bizarre business was suddenly frightening.

Nancy sighed. It was a shuddering sigh and Tux tightened his hold on her, inhaling her delicate aroma of flowers. He hardly remembered moving to comfort her, his protective instincts having risen to the fore, but now he was *very* aware that she felt like heaven itself pressed close to his body.

He could feel her breasts, lush and full, against his chest. He could feel how delicate she was, like fine china. He could feel the tenseness caused by her fright slowly ebbing.

But then there was an even greater shift, change, as senses heightened, as the man totally reacted to the woman, the woman to the man. Heat began to build and churn in a body soft, a body hard. Heartbeats quickened.

The blue shawl, the threatening visions, the endless questions, were all forgotten.

Nancy lifted her head to meet Tux's gaze, seeing the smoky hue of desire in his eyes, not caring if her own eyes revealed the same.

Tux covered her mouth with his, parting her lips, meeting her tongue. It was an explosion of sensation that rocketed through them like the licking flames of a roaring fire.

Hot.

Burning.

He deepened the kiss and passions soared.

Tux raised his head slightly to draw a rough breath, then slanted his mouth the other way as he claimed Nancy's lips again, drinking of her taste like a thirsty man having found sweet nectar.

Oh, Tux, Nancy's mind hummed. It was ecstasy. The feel, the aroma, the taste of this man was exquisite. Never, *never* before had she experienced such an incredible awareness of her own femininity compared to the blatant masculinity of a man, this man, Tux.

She was on fire, burning with the want of him. Her breasts ached with a tantalizing pain, yearning for the soothing touch of Tux's hands. Deep and low within her, the heat pulsed, matching the rapid tempo of her heart.

She was being swept away on passion's tide, and she gloried in it...

What on earth was she doing?

Nancy broke the kiss and moved her hands to press them flat on Tux's chest, pushing him away, forcing him to release her. She took a quick step backward and willed her racing heart to still.

Tux frowned, shook his head once sharply, then took a raspy breath.

"Nancy?" he said, hearing the gritty quality of his voice.

"I..." She wrapped her hands around her elbows. "That shouldn't have happened. I don't do things like that. I don't leap into the arms of a man I don't even know. You must think I'm..." She lifted her chin. "Well, I'm not. Understand? I was upset, momentarily frightened by what you've been saying ever since you came in here."

Tux nodded. "Oh."

"Oh? Oh! That's all you have to say?" she said, none too quietly.

"What do you *want* me to say?" he asked.

"Nothing," she admitted shaking her head. "I'm totally mortified. I don't wish to discuss what happened any further."

"But I just thought of something I want to say."

She glared at him. "Spare me."

"Hang in there," he said, smiling. "This won't take long." His smile faded and his expression became serious. "I just wanted to say that kissing you was sensational. You sent me up in flames, Nancy Shatner. I'm very attracted to you. You're a beautiful, intelligent, passionate woman."

"I am?" She blinked. "I am not! What I mean is, I..." She threw up her hands. "I don't know what I mean. Okay, fine, you've had your say. The subject is closed."

"For now."

"Forever!"

"No way, but we won't argue the point at the moment." He paused. "Listen, like it or not we're in a bit of a mess here." He glanced at the blue shawl **where it** was still spread across the bins of beads, then looked at Nancy again. "The shawl didn't disappear while we were kissing." He stared up at the ceiling, then narrowed his eyes as he directed his attention to the shawl. "Let's gather some data."

Nancy flipped one hand breezily in the air. "Why not? Data is nice. Gather your little heart out."

Tux shot her a dark look, then folded his arms over his chest.

"If I was going to rob this place," he said, "what would I get, besides a life's supply of buttons and beads?"

Nancy shrugged. "Nothing. The majority of my business is mail orders paid by check. The cash flow from walk-in customers is minimal. Tux, seriously, there's nothing here worth stealing."

"Is there a tenant living upstairs?"

"Yes. Me."

He dropped his arms to plant his hands on his narrow hips.

"You're joking. Right? You wouldn't be dumb enough to live alone in this neighborhood. Right? If you do, I just may have to erase the adjective *intelligent* from my list describing you. Tell me you don't live upstairs."

"You're pushing me, Mr. Bishop. This is my store." She pointed to the ceiling. "Up there is my home. That's not dumb, it's sound economic reasoning. I'm a flight of stairs away from my store, which is handy, due to the fact that I can't afford a car. Everything I need is within walking distance of here."

"Including sleazes who would steal from their own grandmothers," Tux said. "This is a high-crime district, lady."

"This is where I live and work, mister. I've been here for nearly two years and I've never had one bit of trouble. We're like a family on this block. We look after each other. No one else has been robbed, or whatever, since I've been here, either, because businesses in this area aren't exactly Fortune 500 enterprises."

"Okay, okay," Tux conceded, raising both hands in a gesture of peace. "You've made your point. Do you own a gun?"

"No."

"Dandy," he muttered, shaking his head. "You don't even have a way to protect yourself. Look, we're not getting anywhere. I think what I should do is talk to someone who's up on psychic powers, see if there's a reasonable explanation for why my friend's have suddenly gone berserk."

"That makes sense. Maybe there's nothing at all to worry about. Maybe Glenna bringing me the blue shawl was just a weird coincidence." She shivered. "Oh, I hope so, I really do."

Tux closed the distance between them and drew one thumb gently over her lips. Nancy shivered again, only this time it wasn't from a sudden rush of fear. The feel of Tux's callused thumb on the soft flesh of her lips had been a simple, quick gesture, yet it had instantaneously fanned the still glowing embers of desire within her into hot, leaping flames.

Tux's friend had sensed she was in danger when he saw his visions? she thought. Tux, himself, was a source of danger to her ability to reason, think straight, behave in a manner she was accustomed to. Oh, yes, Tux Bishop was a very dangerous man.

"I'm sorry about all this, Nancy," he said quietly. "I know I've frightened you, but we'll get to the bottom of it. I'll find out what I can, then report back to you.

"In the meantime, be very careful. Make certain you check the doors and windows at night, don't go strolling outside after dark, things like that. Do you have a telephone upstairs?"

"Yes, it rings up there and down here at the same time. I'll give you one of my business cards with the number." She hurried into the back room and returned to hand him the card, which he slipped into his shirt pocket.

"I'll talk to you soon," he said.

Nancy nodded.

Their eyes met. The sensual haze that had encased them during the kisses shared began to weave its invisible threads once again, over and around them.

The incredible *awareness,* the sensuous pull between them from the moment they'd seen each other was eerie, like nothing either of them had experienced before.

It was exciting, but unsettling.

It was confusing, yet intertwined with a calming *rightness.*

"No," Nancy whispered, not realizing she'd spoken aloud.

"What are you doing to me, Nancy Shatner?" Tux said, his voice raspy.

"Nothing." She took a step backward. "Nothing."

"You look like a beautiful gypsy. Are you? A gypsy? Do you have powers, too, that you haven't told me about?"

"No, of course not. Don't be silly. I'm not a gypsy. I just happen to like to wear this style of clothes sometimes. I get them at Glenna's store."

"Then how do you explain whatever this is that keeps... crackling between us, keeps wrapping around us? I can't find the right words to describe it, but I know you feel it as much as I do. How do you explain that?"

"It's simply a result of the bizarre scenario we're suddenly finding ourselves in," she said. "What am *I* doing to *you?* If you'll recall, Mr. Bishop, *you* came in here with your story of visions and danger, and a blue shawl. *You* started this whole... whatever it is."

A slow smile began to form on Tux's lips, a very male smile, that caused Nancy to take yet another step away from him.

"Well," he replied, "I guess you're right. I started it. The really interesting part will be to see where it all goes. Right, Nancy?"

She lifted her chin. "Goodbye, Tux. I have a great deal of work to do."

He looked at her for another long moment, then nodded.

"I'm off to find an expert on psychic powers. I'll check with you later. Take care of yourself."

Nancy watched as Tux strode from behind the bins to the door, then left the store. Only then did she realize she'd been holding her breath until he was gone, and drew in a gulp of much needed air.

"Oh, goodness," she said, pressing her hands to her cheeks. "What a morning. What a mess. I don't believe this." She turned, then frowned as her gaze fell on the blue shawl. "Yes, I do," she added wearily.

She snatched up the lusciously soft shawl and stomped into the back room.

Late that afternoon, Tux sat in the living room of a seventy-two-year-old man, who looked remarkably like Santa Claus.

"I appreciate your listening to my story, Dr. Nixon," Tux said. "As I explained, I spent most of the day on the telephone looking for help with this situation, and was told more than once that you were the best authority in the area on psychic powers."

"Call me Jeremiah, son," the man answered. "Well, you've brought me an interesting tale, that's for sure. But in all my years of researching psychic phenomena, I've always had to admit the same conclusion…there are no hard-and-fast rules we can count on."

Tux leaned forward, resting his elbows on his knees and lacing his fingers loosely together.

"Can you at least give me your opinion on what has happened?" he asked. "Why did I suddenly have visions predicting the future when I have never before had the power to do that? Even more, how do I know that what I saw will actually take place?"

"The blue shawl has already appeared, son."

Tux slouched back in the chair. "I know." He sighed and shook his head. "I hate this."

Dr. Nixon chuckled. "A person wouldn't need psychic powers to figure *that* out. You obviously like to be in control of your life, and at the moment you feel dictated to by outside forces."

"Exactly. Not only that, there's Nancy Shatner to consider. She's in danger, or will be. But to what degree? I mean, maybe the fear I sensed, then saw on her face in the visions, was because a mouse ran across her floor."

"Good point," Jeremiah agreed, nodding. "It's reasonable to me that your psychic ability took a side trip to an arena where it has never been, but due to your lack of experience, the danger that surrounds Nancy is not easily deciphered."

"I hate this," Tux repeated.

"Well, to be prudent, I'd suggest you assume the worst. Use the cliché of 'better to be safe than sorry.' You'd best watch over Nancy Shatner."

"But for how long? In the first place, it's difficult to continually remember when I'm talking to Nancy that I'm supposedly representing a friend of mine who has the powers, but I sure don't want to tell Nancy the truth. She's already used the word *creepy* in regard to this. I can live without that and the other adjectives she'd come up with. Secondly, I don't know what the danger is, how serious it might be, or how ridiculous."

"True. If she does see a mouse and gets hysterical, then that's the end of the story. But you did say she works and lives in a high-crime neighborhood, so..." Dr. Nixon's voice trailed off.

"Yeah, I hear you," Tux said, frowning.

"Having listened to the details of your background, Tux, you're more than capable of protecting Nancy." He paused. "The lifelong researcher in me is fascinated by all of this. I'm just sorry I can't give you concrete data as to why this happened. All I can offer you is my opinion."

"Which is?"

"I believe that you and Nancy Shatner are connected in some way. The men of science would say that you two had an unexplainable link that enabled you to receive a message from Nancy that was based on events yet to happen."

"Great," Tux said dryly.

"However, there might be another theory coming from the romantics, those who speak more from their hearts than their minds."

"Oh?"

"They'd be inclined to feel that you and Nancy are soul mates, found each other with thoughts before you actually met. She called out to you, you came. Destiny, son, destiny."

"And you? What do *you* believe?"

Dr. Nixon smiled. "I believe I'll be very eager to hear which theory proves to be true. You will keep me posted, won't you?"

Tux got to his feet. "Yes, of course I will, providing I survive it all. I swear, I really—"

"Hate this," Jeremiah concluded for him, laughing. "Tux, the data is crystal clear."

Destiny.

When Dr. Nixon had explained the two approaches to viewing the situation, Tux had filed the information and not paid active attention to it.

But as he drove away from the old gentleman's house, he realized he was actually *hearing* for the first time that portion of what had been said.

Destiny.

Destiny?

Ah, come on, give it a rest, Tux thought, with an impatient shake of his head. That really was the nonsense of romantics.

Soul mates.

He was chucking that one out the window, too. He and Nancy Shatner were *not* soul mates, not each other's destiny.

That was a bunch of hogwash. He and Nancy had connected by thought waves because they hadn't yet met as they were *destined* to do? Ridiculous.

But...

Nancy had called out to him.

And he'd come.

She was in some kind of potential danger.

He fully intended to watch over and protect her until the source of that danger could be discovered and dealt with.

He'd been determined to locate the beautiful, gypsylike woman, who had pleaded for help in his visions.

And when he *did* find her, he'd kissed her.

Tux tightened his hold on the steering wheel and shifted slightly on the seat as heat coiled low and tight in his body from the remembrance of the kisses shared with Nancy.

She'd turned him inside out, that was for sure. He'd *never* been so instantly consumed by lust when kissing a woman.

"Wrong," he said, smacking the steering wheel with the heel of his hand.

It hadn't been just lust. What had swept throughout him like a hot, flaming rocket when he'd held Nancy in his arms, kissed her, savored the feel of her feminine, delicate body nestled against him, had *not* been just lust.

There had been a maze of indiscernible emotions tumbling through his mind as well. He'd recognized protectiveness and possessiveness, but the remainder were a tangled puzzle.

Protectiveness? That was easily explained. Nancy was in some kind of danger from an event yet to take place. It was perfectly natural for a decent, basically nice guy, to be determined to protect her from that danger lurking in future shadows.

Possessiveness? Well, that was reasonable, too. After all, he was the one who had been mentally informed of that danger, then delivered the news flash of its existence to Nancy. She was his for the duration of this dilemma; his to protect. His. Hence, the emotion of possessiveness.

Tux nodded decisively.

Destiny? Soul mates? Forget it. He was a realist, a man who operated with his feet firmly on the ground.

Logical thinking dictated that romantic-based psychic messages could only be received by someone who had a mind receptive to those kinds of thoughts, a place to receive them.

That wasn't him, not by a long shot. Therefore, he was back to Dr. Nixon's theory one, the scientific analysis. By some cosmic...or whatever...fluke, his brain waves had mistakenly connected with Nancy's. It was like dialing the telephone and getting the wrong number.

There, he decided, he had at least some of this disaster figured out, and felt better for it. The fact remained though, that he was well and truly stuck with the situation itself, had to see it through to its proper end.

He'd protect Nancy Shatner.

Because, for now, she was his.

Fine.

Tux turned on the radio and began to sing along to a country-and-western song declaring that mamas shouldn't let their babies grow up to be cowboys.

"Whoa," he said suddenly, "I'm supposed to be at Mom and Dad's house for dinner."

He flicked on the blinker, changed lanes, and concentrated on the heavy traffic.

He totally ignored the whispering little voice in his mind that repeated one word over and over...*destiny.*

In her apartment above Buttons and Beads, Nancy set a salad and a plate of toast on the table next to a tall glass of iced tea. She sank wearily onto a wobbly wooden chair and sighed.

The remainder of the day after Tux had left the store had

seemed like a never-going-to-end series of hours. She'd had difficulty concentrating, and had to continually recount piles of beads as she lost track of what number she was on.

Images of what had taken place with Tux Bishop kept flitting before her mind's eye from every direction.

She saw him frowning, then smiling that sinfully lethal smile, saw desire in the mesmerizing depths of his incredible blue eyes.

She saw herself in his arms, responding to his kisses in total abandon, her behavior far removed from her normal conduct.

And she saw the bright blue shawl.

Nancy picked up a slice of toast, glared at it, then dropped it back onto the plate. She got to her feet and crossed the small room to look out the window, her gaze sweeping over as much of the block as she could see.

Was there really something, someone, out there intent on doing her harm? Was she in danger from a source unknown?

Oh, if only she could turn back the clock, erase the moment that Tux had opened the door and entered Buttons and Beads, and remove this nightmare from her life.

But if she had the power to do that, she would never have experienced the ecstasy of kissing Tux, being held by him, savoring the wonderful feel of his magnificent, strong body pressed against her.

"Nancy," she said dismally, "you're a befuddled mess."

She continued to stare out the window, her hands wrapped around her elbows.

She was tired, confused and frightened.

Two tears slid down her pale cheeks.

And for the first time in a long while, she was very, very lonely.

Three

When Tux entered the living room at his parents' home, Blue and Bram were already there.

"Yo, big brother," Blue called. "Do any cloak-and-dagger investigating today?"

"You could say that," Tux replied, no hint of a smile on his face. "Punch any cows?"

Bram laughed. "He gotcha good, Blue. Before anyone asks... Yes, today I worked on building a building. Bishop Construction is alive and well, thank you very much."

The brothers were all six feet tall, with well-proportioned physiques. They boasted the same shade of blue eyes, which most women commented on shortly after meeting them. Their features were similar: rugged, handsome, tanned, definitely declaring them to be related, but each uniquely their own.

But it was the contrasting shades of their hair that was immediately apparent when the three were together.

While Tux's hair was blond and sun-streaked to nearly

white in places, Blue's was as black as a raven's wing, causing his eyes to appear even a deeper, richer shade of sapphire. Bram's shade of hair fell somewhere in between his brothers, being medium brown, with some sun-lightened streaks.

They were the Bishop boys, and each knew his brothers would lay their lives on the line for him.

Tux slouched into a green-and-red plaid chair that Jana-John had bought at a yard sale over twenty years before, deciding it was a "happy chair." No one had questioned her as to how a chair could look "happy." The now rather faded, lumpy creation had been set in place and never moved from the selected spot for two decades.

"You don't look too happy, Tux," Bram said, from where he sat on a blue-and-white striped sofa.

"Mmm," Tux murmured.

Blue settled onto an old Boston rocker that Jana-John had used for countless hours to rock her babies.

"So?" Blue prompted. "Are you talking about it, Tux, or just mulling over whatever is eating at you? Your call, my man."

"Where are the folks?" Tux asked.

Blue and Bram both shrugged.

"They'll pop up," Bram said, "providing they remember we're here for dinner. I don't smell anything cooking, though." He smiled. "Which is safer, really. Maybe we'll send out for pizza."

"Hold that thought," Blue said. "Pray that thought. We've got the greatest mother in Texas…hell, the world…but heaven knows she can't cook. Hey, remember the time she decided to make us pancakes from scratch?"

"Yep," Bram said, chuckling. "We sold them to every kid on the block. Twenty-five cents for a homemade, rock-hard Frisbee."

Bram looked at Tux, who was staring into space, glowering at nothing.

"Okay, Tux," Bram said. "I guess you'd better spill it before you explode."

"I hate this," Tux muttered. "I really hate this."

"Hate what?" Blue and Bram said in unison.

Tux got to his feet and began to pace restlessly around the room that had been carpeted in a striped pattern of fuchsia, yellow and black.

"I had a vision," Tux told them. "Correct that. I had *three* visions in as many nights. I didn't meditate, didn't concentrate, didn't go into a near-trance. The visions just came on their own."

"That has never happened before," Blue said.

"It gets worse," Tux continued, still pacing around the room. "It turns out that the visions were predicting the future, not showing something in the present."

"Whew," Bram said. "You don't *have* the ability to predict the future. We checked that out years ago when we were planning to bet five bucks on a Super Bowl."

"Yeah, well, I saw the future. A woman...an incredibly beautiful woman...named Nancy Shatner, who owns a store called Buttons and Beads, is in some kind of danger. I sensed the danger, but I don't know how serious it is, or what the danger is from. I saw her in the visions pleading for help, crying, and she was wearing a bright blue shawl."

"Define *incredibly beautiful*," Bram said, but his brothers ignored him.

"Did you track her down?" Blue asked. "Does she own a blue shawl?"

Tux stopped and shoved both hands through his thick hair.

"Are you ready for this?" he said. "While I'm standing in her store, trying to convince her that my *friend,* who had the visions, isn't totally nuts, a lady from down the block, who has a used clothes place, bounces in all excited because she's bringing Nancy a bright blue shawl she knows Nancy will want to have."

"Holy smokes," Bram uttered, his eyes widening.

"No joke," Blue said. "Is this for real? You don't have *any* clue as to what kind of danger Incredibly Beautiful Nancy is in?"

"Obviously not," Jana-John said, coming into the room. "Therefore, you'd better watch over Nancy Shatner until this mystery is solved, Tux."

Blue and Bram had gotten to their feet the instant their mother appeared.

Jana-John Bishop was just barely over five feet tall and had an ethereal aura. She seemed to *float* when she walked, just glided gracefully when she moved from one place to the next.

Her blue eyes were clear and sparkling, her features those of her sons, but softened to feminine perfection. Her blond hair was swept to the top of her head and secured by two combs. The hairdo had taken her moments to arrange, and looked like she'd spent hours in a beauty salon to achieve the fetching, tousled affect.

Tonight she was wearing a flowing "something" that had been crafted from a multitude of filmy handkerchiefs.

When the boys were small, one of their friends had asked them, "How come you got a fairy princess for a mom, and I only got a regular kinda mom?"

"Hello, my darlings," Jana-John said, kissing each on the cheek as they bent down so she could reach them. "Oh, you're all so handsome, so fine." She looked at Tux. "You're disturbed by what has happened with your psychic powers, aren't you, dear? I heard you talking while I was putting dinner on the table.

"Bram, go retrieve your father from his study, and we'll discuss Tux's problem while we eat."

Tall, thin, Abraham Lincoln Bishop soon took his place at the head of the table. He'd fastened his shirt one button off, leaving it lopsided, and his dark hair stood straight up from long fingers being pulled through it during the day.

He had a generally disheveled appearance and a bemused expression on his face. But when he met each of his sons' gaze, Abe's light blue eyes radiated warmth and love.

"Good evening, darling wife," Abe said, looking at Jana-John. "You look exquisite this evening."

"Thank you, love," she said, smiling.

She settled onto her chair at the opposite end of the table from her husband, and clasped her hands beneath her chin.

"Isn't this a delightful meal for a hot summer night?" she said. "There's lemonade, sliced smoked chicken from the deli, two loaves of crunchy French bread, and a delicious fruit salad."

"Marvelous, my dear," Abe said, beaming.

Tux, Blue and Bram looked at the six bowls on the table. There was one filled with oranges, another held apples, then on they went—bananas, grapes, peaches and plums.

"Fruit salad?" Blue said.

"Well, yes," his mother said. "Arrange the fruit on your plate, take a bite of each in whatever order you prefer, and by the time it all reaches your tummy, you'll have a salad."

Bram shrugged. "Makes sense to me." He tossed an orange to Tux. Tux's hand shot out and snatched the orange out of the air. "Start your salad, big brother."

They ate in silence for a few minutes, then Jana-John explained to Abe what had taken place with Tux's psychic powers.

"You don't say," Abe said. "Tux, you see that you take proper care of that young woman until this mystery is solved."

"Yes, sir," Tux said.

"He knows that, Abe," Jana-John said. "In all your reading have you run across anything like this?"

"Can't remember that I have," Abe said. "Back in history if a man had psychic powers they locked him away in an institution."

"Good plan," Blue said. "Bye, Tux. Can I have your stereo system?"

Tux glared at Blue, then directed his attention to his father. "I spoke to a Dr. Jeremiah Nixon this afternoon about this mess."

"Nixon, Nixon," Abe mused. "Ah, yes, he's the expert on psychic phenomena. What did he have to say?"

"He had a couple of theories," Tux said. "He could only offer his opinion, because the whole area of psychic powers is impossible to set into hard-and-fast rules."

"What were Dr. Nixon's theories, Tux dear?" Jana-John asked.

"The one that made the most sense was that Nancy's and my thought waves accidently connected."

"That's boring," Bram said. "Let's hear the theory that didn't make sense."

Destiny. "No," Tux said. *Soul mates.* "It's not worth discussing. Look, I appreciate all of your support, but there's no point in hashing this over. All I can do is wait and see what happens."

"And..." Jana-John prompted.

"Watch over..." Abe said.

"Take care of..." Bram said.

"Nancy Shatner," Blue said.

"Got it," Tux said. "Blue, give me a banana, please. My fruit salad is lacking something here."

Jana-John sighed. "Tux, I heard you say that you told Nancy a friend of yours had seen the visions. I do so wish you'd accept your special gift and be comfortable with it. It's nothing to be secretive or embarrassed about."

"Mom," Tux said, "we've had this discussion since I was a kid. I'm not about to change my stand on the subject now. I've revealed my powers on enough occasions to know the reaction to me is negative."

"But you're not being totally honest with Nancy Shatner," Jana-John said.

Tux shrugged. "Close enough. I *am* my own friend, you know. Please, let's drop it. Okay?"

"Yes, all right," Jana-John conceded, sighing again.

The rather unusual dinner completed, everyone served themselves up huge bowls of ice cream. The Bishop home had never once been without ice cream.

"Now then," Jana-John said, "how are you three doing in your search for wives? It has been over four months since we all sat around this table and you boys said you wanted to get married and have babies. Any progress in the two weeks since you were here for dinner?"

"No," her sons answered in unison.

"Back in history," Abe told them, "your brides would have been chosen by your father."

Yeah, well, Tux thought dryly, that held more appeal than having a woman come into a guy's life through a psychic fluke.

"It may come to that, Dad," Blue said, shaking his head. "I can't believe how difficult it is to find a wife. None of us have ever been short on female company, but those women sure do seem different when you squint your eyes and envision them as the mother of your children, your partner until death do you part."

"That's the truth," Bram agreed, frowning. "I'm getting nowhere very quickly. It's totally depressing."

"Dad," Tux said, smiling at Abe, "I'm beginning to believe that you captured the heart of the last lady on earth fit to marry, sir."

"Hush with you," Jana-John said, blushing prettily. "You boys aren't giving up, are you? You still want to marry and have babies, don't you?"

All three nodded decisively.

"I'm ready to settle down and settle in," Tux said. "We

all are. We figured we'd fill this house with kids when we came to visit. But, man, this finding a wife is one tough number."

"Back in history..." Abe said.

"Yes, dear, we know," Jana-John intoned gently. "Tux, Blue, Bram, you've simply got to concentrate harder on finding wives. I've already started painting pictures for the nurseries."

"Oh, Lord," Blue muttered.

"Somewhere out there," Jana-John said, "are three lovely young women, who are meant to be the brides of my three wonderful sons. Oh, yes, they're waiting for you. They're your soul mates, your destinies."

Tux choked on a spoonful of ice cream. Bram was only too happy to pound him on the back until Tux yelled for mercy.

Nancy was jarred from a deep sleep before dawn the next morning by the shrill ringing of the telephone.

She snapped on the lamp sitting on the nightstand next to the bed, threw back the sheet and swung her feet to the floor in the same motion.

After leaving the bedroom, she hurried across the dark living room, hoping she wouldn't bump into anything on the way.

Relying on memory as to where the telephone rested on the end table by the sofa, she snatched up the receiver.

"Yes? Hello?" she said breathlessly.

"Nancy?"

Stifling a groan of frustration, Nancy sank onto the sofa. "Mother, it's not even five o'clock yet. Is something wrong?"

"No, no, nothing is wrong. I've been up for quite a while, had my tea, read the newspaper, and was thinking about you. You haven't telephoned me, and you know how that distresses me. It's not kind of you, Nancy, it really isn't."

"This is Wednesday," Nancy said, struggling to be patient. "Very early on Wednesday. You and I spoke on Sunday."

"Well, I still don't see why you won't phone every day. I know it's long-distance rates from Texas to Florida, but I said you should call collect. If your father was still alive, rest his soul, he'd insist you call home every day. Is it too much for a mother to ask?"

"Mother, there's no reason to run up an enormous telephone bill by calling each day. Once a week is enough to get caught up on our news."

"That's not the point. I worry so much about you when I think of you living in that awful neighborhood. I probably shouldn't have come to visit you last year and seen how horrible it is there."

Nancy did not reply, just waited for the rest of the lecture.

"How you can continue to cause me such upset by insisting on staying there, I'll just never know. We have such a lovely place right here where you could be safe and sound in the home you grew up in. I deserve better than this, Nancy."

And I deserve to have a life, Nancy thought wearily. She'd had this conversation so many times, she'd lost count. She loved her mother, she truly did, but Ruth Shatner, and her father as well when he'd been alive, had kept a stranglehold on her, smothered her.

Her mother had become even worse since Kenneth Shatner had passed away three years ago. Ruth simply refused to accept the fact that her daughter was a grown woman, an independent woman, who had every right to live her life as she saw fit.

Ruth continually attempted to convince Nancy to move back to Florida. When that plea failed, she'd try to make Nancy feel guilty about living so far away, wanted her to telephone daily, *wanted her to be accountable for practically every minute of her life.*

"Nancy?"

"I'm here, Mother. Did you investigate doing some volunteer work like I suggested?"

"No, I'm not certain I can take on something like that at my age. You forget all the time that I didn't give birth to you..."

Until I was forty-two, Nancy silently supplied.

"...until I was forty-two," Ruth said.

We'd given up hope of ever having a child, Nancy mused absently, twirling the telephone cord around her finger.

"We'd given up hope of ever having a child," Ruth rambled on, "then..."

"There I was," Nancy said aloud, "such a blessing, such a joy."

"Well, yes. Not only that, but your father and I realized it meant we'd have companionship in our old age, a loving daughter to be with us in the winter of our years." Ruth sniffled. "Now I've lost your father *and* you. How can you do this to me, Nancy? Don't you believe you owe your own mother some loving-kindness?"

"I *owe* it to myself to be an independent adult and live my life the way I choose to." Nancy sighed. "Mother, we've been over this and over this a hundred times. I'm *not* moving back to Florida. I'm *not* giving up Buttons and Beads. I'm *not* leaving this apartment. I'm *not* going to call you every day."

"Watch the tone of voice you use with me, young lady. I certainly didn't allow you to be rude while you were under my roof."

You didn't allow me to breathe! "I'm sorry, Mother. I'm not my best before I've had some coffee."

"Coffee isn't good for you. I read a study on it. You should have hot tea in the morning."

"Good idea. I'll go brew some tea right now. I'll talk to you over the weekend. All right? Great. Have a super day. I love you, Mother."

"But..."

"Bye-bye, for now." Nancy quickly replaced the receiver.

Leaning her head back on the top of the faded sofa, she closed her eyes.

Oh, dear heaven, the situation with her mother was so difficult to deal with. It was as though they'd reversed roles; the mother having become the child, the child now being the mother.

It was a constant struggle not to feel guilty, not to crumble under the burden of responsibility for happiness her mother continually heaped on her.

Darn it, it wasn't fair. She, Nancy Shatner, had every right to be independent, live her own life, *be free*. She'd remain strong, would not allow Ruth to chip, chip, chip away at her. The days of Ruth controlling her daughter's every move were over.

Nancy lifted her head. "I will *never* be accountable to anyone but myself ever again. Not to a mother, father, or to a man who might attempt to be part of my life!"

She stiffened as the image of Tux Bishop suddenly appeared in her mental vision, so clearly there she felt as though she could actually reach out and touch him.

"Shoo," she said, flapping one hand in the air. "Go away."

How strange, she thought, to think of Tux Bishop when thinking of people who wanted to smother her.

Did that make sense? No, it certainly didn't. Well, maybe it did. Sort of. Tux *was* the only eligible man she knew.

She hadn't had a date since moving to Texas over two years ago, as she didn't have a way to meet people beyond the neighborhood due to the lack of a car. The people she knew were all senior citizens.

But Tux hadn't entered her life as a potential boyfriend. He'd come as the bearer of bad news with his dire predictions of danger and a bright blue shawl.

He wasn't a threat to her independence; he wasn't looking to date her. He saw her as a stress-producing by-product of a psychic glitch, or some such thing, that a friend of his had experienced.

Then again, he *had* said she was beautiful and that he was attracted to her.

And those kisses they'd shared?

Oh, my, those kisses had been ecstasy. They'd curled her toes, melted her bones, and...

Nancy jumped to her feet as she felt a sudden swish of heat begin to thrum low in her body.

Enough of Tux Bishop, she thought, starting across the now sun-filled room. He'd exit stage left as soon as the mystery surrounding the whys and wherefores of the unwelcomed visions had been solved.

Tux was only a threat if she allowed him to be, which she *would not.* She'd have to stay alert, though, because the blatantly masculine, charming, sexy, handsome-beyond-belief, kisser-extraordinaire Mr. Bishop, had the *potential* to be threatening to her independent life-style.

She mustn't forget for a single second that Tux was a *very* dangerous man.

"Coffee," she said aloud. "I need coffee. Not tea. Coffee."

Bishop Investigations was located on the fourth floor of a tall building in downtown Houston. The rent was astronomical, the furnishings Tux had chosen had cost him a bundle, as had the computers, fax and copying machine. He also had a vast array of high-tech equipment to facilitate carrying out to its proper end almost anything a client might request done.

Two of his investigators were in their early forties and had been agents, one was a thirty-year-old former police officer. His secretary was a middle-aged widow of a police officer who had been killed in the line of duty.

When he'd retired from the agency, Tux had squinted his eyes at his investment portfolio, converted two thirds of it into cash, and started Bishop Investigations.

His reasoning, he'd explained to his family, was to look prosperous and sought after from day one, thus hopefully attracting clients from the get-go.

Tux's approach had been sound, and Bishop Investigations had been operating in the black from nearly the beginning. He was seriously considering hiring another investigator to handle the ever-increasing cases coming their way.

The only thing that was slightly out of sync with the posh surroundings in the office, was the apparel of the staff. Tux refused to wear a suit and tie, and didn't ask his investigators to. However, the jeans, khakis, chinos, or whatever, worn by the staff, had seemed to enhance the image of being so top-notch they were in a position to do as they darned well pleased.

As Tux rode up in the elevator to the fourth floor, he thought yet again about the fact that he'd had a solid night's sleep.

Why? he asked himself for the umpteenth time, since awakening at dawn. Why had the visions of Nancy, the danger surrounding her, the blue shawl, suddenly stopped after annoying him three nights in a row?

Damn, he wished there were more concrete facts on record, having been researched and determined to be true by men like Dr. Nixon. So much of the data on psychic phenomena was guesswork.

So, *guess,* Bishop, he told himself, as he left the elevator and walked down the carpeted corridor. He *guessed* that once he brought the mental images into an arena of reality by finding Nancy, Buttons and Beads and the bright blue shawl, he'd...what? Short-circuited? Hung up the mental telephone? Turned off the link of the future to his psychic channel?

Hell, he didn't know. As much as he hated, *really hated,* receiving visions from the future, he'd halfway wished he'd seen more last night. What a relief it would have been to glimpse the mouse that scared Nancy Shatner while she was wearing the bright blue shawl.

The mystery could have been instantly solved, and that would be that.

He'd never see Nancy again.

Tux stopped in front of his office and frowned, not reaching for the doorknob.

Never see Nancy again?

Well, yeah, that was the ultimate goal. He wanted this unsettling mess figured out, taken care of and forgotten. That included Nancy and her blue shawl.

So why did the thought of never seeing Nancy again cause a knot to tighten in his gut?

Okay, he was attracted to her. And, yes, kissing her had been fantastic, the explosive sensual reactions *not* just lust.

But he was a man in charge of his own life, his own *destiny*. And he was a *Texas* man, who followed the code of doing things *his* way.

He didn't care how much he desired Nancy, how the mere remembrance of the kisses shared, her feminine aroma, the feel of her delicate body nestled to his, turned him inside out and created burning flames of passions that licked throughout him.

He wasn't becoming physically, nor emotionally, involved with a woman who had been thrust into his life by his psychic powers.

Yes, he wanted a life's partner and, yes, he wanted to create babies with that special woman.

But because of the way he'd met Nancy, the circumstances surrounding his being in close proximity with her, Nancy Shatner was not, nor would she ever be, a candidate for being his future wife.

With a decisive nod, Tux opened the door and entered the office.

Two minutes before five o'clock that evening, Nancy started toward the door of Buttons and Beads to lock it. She stopped in her tracks as Tux entered, snapped the lock into place, then flipped the sign to read Closed.

He turned to look at Nancy, folded his arms across his chest and frowned.

"We're going out to dinner," he said, "so I can bring you up-to-date on what I found out about psychic powers going haywire. Then I'll tell you how we're tackling this, what the plan is, exactly what you're to do and not do. Get your purse. Oh, and bring the blue shawl."

Fury rushed through Nancy like a current of a wild river. She planted tightened fists on her hips, narrowed her eyes, and her voice quivered with anger when she spoke.

"Don't you *ever* tell me what to do. I don't take orders from you, or anyone. Is that clear? I'm an independent woman, who answers to no one but myself. Have you got that? You have three seconds to get out of my store and out of my life. *Forever.*"

Four

Oh, man, Tux thought. He'd blown it by marching in there barking orders. Well, no problem. He'd just turn on the ever-famous Bishop charm and soothe Nancy's ruffled feathers.

He took a deep breath, then let it out slowly as he stared up at the ceiling. When he looked at Nancy again, he held up both hands in a gesture of peace, having produced his best smile at full power.

"I humbly apologize, Ms. Shatner," he said, still smiling. "I had a rotten day, but that's no excuse for being rude, or for telling you what to do."

He crossed his arms loosely over his chest.

"Therefore," he continued pleasantly, "I'm requesting the honor of your company at dinner, so I can inform you of what I've discovered about psychic powers. We will also, with your permission, discuss the best plan of action for tackling our present dilemma."

He nodded, the smile still firmly in place.

"All right?" he said. "Certainly. Now, if you'll be so kind as to get your purse and *please* bring the blue shawl with you, we'll be on our way."

Nancy looked directly at him, her fists still planted on her hips.

"No," she said, absolutely no hint of a smile on *her* face.

Tux's smile disappeared instantly, and was replaced by an expression of total confusion.

"What?" he said, an incredulous tone to his voice.

"No, I won't go to dinner with you. No, I don't feel like discussing the weather, let alone the screwy situation you've dumped on me."

She narrowed her eyes.

"I saw you shift gears, Tux Bishop. You just pushed a button and oozed charm. You must associate with bubble-brain women if that routine has worked for you in the past. I'm not falling for your malarkey. It's despicable."

Tux tried another smile and Nancy rolled her eyes heavenward. "Oh, please...give it a rest."

Tux frowned and ran one hand over the back of his neck. He dropped his hand and shook his head.

"Where are my brothers when I need them?" he muttered. "I could use some advice here."

"There's more than one of you? Heaven help the female populace."

"Well, yeah, I have twin brothers, Blue and Bram. They're about a year younger than I am. Great guys. You'd really like them." He paused. "Well, you probably wouldn't like them in the frame of mind you're in, but they *are* good men. My parents are fantastic, too. Do you have family, Nancy?"

"Just a mother, who lives in Florida. Your mother had three babies in diapers? Goodness, she must have been exhausted all the time."

Tux shrugged. "She says she loved those years." He laughed. "One time, when we three boys were small, a man came to the house to spray for bugs. He stepped into the living room and got all upset, asked my mom if she'd called the police because our house had obviously been trashed by vandals.

"My mom just smiled and said she just hadn't gotten around to picking up the place lately, because she'd been playing with her baby boys. The clutter could keep, she said, but childhood was gone far too fast to miss any of it. She's something, my mom, a very special lady."

"You're fortunate to have a mother like that," Nancy said softly.

"Yeah, I know. My dad is wonderful, too. He's a bit absentminded, but all of us know he'd come through in a flash if we needed him."

He sighed.

"Nancy, look, I'm sorry, I really am, about the way I came in here. We do need to talk, and I thought it would be nice to share a meal while we discussed the things that we have to go over. Okay?"

Nancy looked at him for a long moment, then smiled as she nodded.

"Okay. I apologize, too. I'm a tad oversensitive about being told what to do, I guess. I'll get my purse."

"And the blue shawl. Please."

"And the blue shawl."

She turned and started across the room.

"Nancy?"

She stopped and glanced back at Tux over her shoulder. "Yes?"

"We had an argument and made up, just like the grown-ups. How about that?"

"Yes," she said, smiling at him warmly. "How about that?"

Their eyes met.

The moment was quiet, peaceful, like blessed silence after a raging storm.

The moment held a message sent and received of a better understanding and a measure of trust.

The moment would be remembered.

Tux had a low-slung, candy-apple red sports car that he told Nancy with a burst of laughter was what he drove when he was doing his "male thing." His vehicle that made sense, he explained, was a Blazer.

"I'm showing off with this baby," he admitted, patting the steering wheel, "so stroke my male ego and be impressed to the state of awe."

"At least you're honest about it," Nancy said, laughing in delight at his candor. "Okay, sir, I am, indeed, duly impressed."

Their mingled laughter filled the car and cascaded over Nancy and Tux like a refreshing mist from a crystal clear waterfall.

Oh, how glorious it was, Nancy thought, wiggling even farther into the butter soft leather of the bucket seat, to feel young and happy, to be laughing right out loud over nonsense that was just plain fun. It had been so long, so very long, since she'd felt so *free*.

"Now tell me, Nancy," Tux said, bringing her from her thoughts, "how did you come to start a business as unusual as Buttons and Beads?"

"I was a business major in college in Florida and I had no idea what I was going to do with my degree after I graduated. I ended up a class short in my senior year, so I picked one out of a hat. It was a course called The History of Ordinary Things."

"Interesting. And?"

"Did you know that the Chinese people invented playing cards, umbrellas, paper and printing?"

"I'll be darned. Playing cards?"

"Yep. When the professor got to the section on beads, I can remember thinking it was going to be boring. It wasn't, not even close, and by the end of the course I was hooked on beads and all the complexities associated with them.

"I decided that was the kind of business I would have. I added buttons to my store just for fun, but there are an amazing number of people who collect buttons of all kinds. As far as beads go, I learned that— Do you really want to hear this?"

Tux nodded. "Yes, I do. This is fascinating."

And Nancy was fascinating, he mused. Nancy was also, as he'd told his brothers, incredibly beautiful.

She was wearing navy blue slacks that accentuated her shapely bottom and slender legs.

Her pale blue overblouse was cinched at the waist...a tiny, very feminine waist...with a belt made from blue beads with felt ties.

That wild tumble of hair, those silky black waves, were making his hands tingle with the urge to sift it through his fingers. Sensational.

Her dark eyes were sparkling, her voice was animated. She was so alive, so vibrant.

Incredibly Beautiful Nancy Shatner.

"Beads have a language all their own," Nancy informed him. "In ancient times if a man wore a necklace, or wrist and ankle bracelets made by stringing together lion's teeth, he was praying for the strength and bravery of the lion. If he strung seeds, he was hoping for a good harvest.

"People of different origins often learned to communicate with each other by presenting various beads, or things used as beads, that had universal meaning."

"Beads became money, too," Tux said. "Right?"

"Ah, yes. Who can forget that Manhattan Island was bought for twenty-four dollars' worth of trade beads. At one time, the technology of making trade beads was a highly guarded secret. After all, they were money.''

"Go on," Tux prompted, nodding. "This is really great stuff."

"There are beads to divert the evil eye, and another kind called Ghost Beads. They're given as gifts to women to protect them, bringing them happiness, and a long and loving marriage. Colors are important, too."

"Why?"

"Well, there are people who buy beads from me in shades to match something they own. Others place orders for specific colors because they've studied the history of beads and the meaning of their colors.

"For example, black beads are for protection, supposedly absorb negative influences. White is for strength. A very bright red gives courage and confidence. The list goes on and on."

"That belt you're wearing is made of blue beads. What does that mean?"

"Serenity, truth, good health, harmony. Blue was very popular in the late forties and early fifties, and is once again in vogue now. Blue is the special color for Monday, the Hopeful Day."

"No joke? Okay, this is Wednesday. Does it have a special color?"

"Oh, yes. Wednesday is yellow for Wisdom Day."

"My folks are going to love hearing all this," Tux said. "My dad is really into anything that can be prefaced by 'back in history.' So, you're wearing blue. You must be feeling serene, you're telling the truth, and you're in good health. Blue gets a lot of jobs done."

"We're talking folklore here, you realize."

"Yeah," Tux said, suddenly frowning, "we have a blue shawl that is definitely not contributing to our serenity. I guess the good-news-blue only applies to beads."

Nancy sighed. "Well, back to reality. The ever-famous blue shawl."

"Reality? Hell, it's *our* reality, but the whole situation is unreal." Tux paused. "There's a steak house up ahead that serves delicious food. Does that strike your fancy?"

"Yes, that's fine," Nancy answered quietly.

It was just as well that Tux had shattered the lighthearted mood, she decided. She'd been enjoying herself so much, had been chattering away like any woman would who was out on a date with a handsome, charming man, who gave every indication that he was truly interested in what she had to say.

But this wasn't a social event. It was a business meeting of sorts, so that Tux could report on what he'd discovered regarding the unexpected psychic glimpse his friend had had of the future, and to present a plan to deal with it.

That Tux Bishop was the most incredibly masculine and compelling man she'd ever met wasn't important in the overall scheme of things. They were together to hopefully solve the mystery of the bizarre situation they were involved in, nothing more.

Nothing, she told herself, *more*.

Between the time that Tux found a place to park, they'd walked across the lot, then entered the restaurant, Nancy had had a slight shift in her mind-set.

This was the first time, she mused, in the two-plus years since she'd moved to Texas, that she'd spent the evening in the company of a man.

The drive from her store to the steak house had been such fun. But now she was in a gloomy mood, because of the subject matter she and Tux had to sift and sort through.

Well, drat. She wasn't ready to give up her cheerful frame of mind. Where was it written that she couldn't continue to enjoy the evening, as long as she remembered the reason she and Tux were there?

She wouldn't forget that this wasn't a date. But couldn't she still savor being out to dinner, couldn't she enjoy the conversation and sharing, instead of spending the evening alone in the silence of her little apartment?

Well, sure. Why not? She understood the facts, rules, the boundaries of these few hours. Therefore she was going to have a marvelous time.

They were seated at a small table with a candle in the center set in an old-fashioned hurricane lamp. The restaurant was casual, with a rustic motif that included sawdust on the floor and waitresses in red-and-white checked gingham dresses.

After ordering steaks, baked potatoes and salads, Tux looked at Nancy with every intention of beginning his report by telling her of his conversation with Dr. Nixon.

What the soft glow of candlelight did for Nancy wasn't fair, he thought instead. Her skin had an ivory velvet appearance, her dark hair and eyes shone like polished ebony. Her lips… Damn, he was a dying man.

"I…" he began, then cleared his throat. "Would you like me to move that candle to the side of the table? Those types of hurricane tops sometimes cause candles to smoke too much."

"Oh, no, it's fine," Nancy said, smiling.

Also fine, she thought, was gazing at Tux as the candlelight accentuated his rugged features, his tan and those gorgeous blue eyes of his.

"You're positive you don't want me to move the candle?" Tux asked. *Please, Nancy? Give me a break.*

"*Very* positive."

"Oh."

"This is a nice restaurant," she commented pleasantly. "It's cute, comfy and cozy. Do you see that woman over there wearing purple? That color denotes mystery, the unknown. Hmm, I wonder what her secret is?"

"The color that should be on our minds," Tux said, frowning, "is blue, as in the blue shawl that's draped over the back of your chair."

"Oh, yes, of course, the shawl." Nancy paused. "Maybe that woman is a government agent, like you used to be. Were there women in your rank and file?"

Tux nodded. "Absolutely. They were top-notch. They—" He stopped and shook his head. "Enough. The shawl?"

"The blue shawl. That would be a great title for a book. *The Mystery of the Blue Shawl.* Or *The Magic of the Blue Shawl.* Or *The Blue Shawl Mystery.* Or—"

"Nancy," Tux interrupted, frowning, "are you getting hysterical?"

"Of course not," she said, smoothing the napkin over her lap. "I just don't see why we have to be so terribly serious all the time about this situation."

"It's serious business," he said, much too loudly. He glanced quickly around, then lowered his voice when he spoke again. "You do recall that danger was sensed in all three of the visions my friend had, don't you? Catch the operative word, Nancy...*danger.*"

"Mmm," she said, nodding. "Oh, here are our salads. Don't they look scrumptious?"

"Remind me to tell you sometime about the fruit salad I had at my folks' house last night. It was what is known as an 'experience.'"

Nancy took a bite of crisp lettuce, then looked at Tux questioningly.

"How can an ordinary fruit salad be an...experience?" she said.

As Tux explained his mother's rationale of how to produce a perfectly fine fruit salad once it all hit a person's stomach, he realized he was powerless to curb his smile.

Nancy's eyes were actually sparkling as she laughed in delight at the description of the meal he'd shared with his family the previous night.

Nancy was like a breath of fresh air, he mused, a summer breeze, a field of untouched, vibrant wildflowers, a... Good Lord, he sounded like a corny poet.

But, darn it, her smile and laughter were infectious, her honest, open demeanor a welcome change from the game-playing women he knew.

Oh, yes, Nancy Shatner was a spell weaver, all right. They were already halfway through eating their salads, and they hadn't addressed one detail of why they were actually there.

Get a grip, Bishop, he ordered himself. *Right now.*

He pushed his plate to one side and folded his arms on top of the table, leaning slightly toward Nancy.

"Okay, listen up," he said gruffly.

Nancy raised one eyebrow. "I beg your pardon?"

He rolled his eyes heavenward. "Okay, listen up...*please.* I'm not *telling* you to listen up, I'm *asking* you to listen up."

"Oh," she said, nodding. "Fine. Proceed."

"Thanks so much," he said dryly.

"There's no cause to get grumpy, Tux."

He counted slowly to ten in his mind, then decided he was once again calm, cool and collected.

"You're right," he said. "Now then, I spoke with an expert on the subject of psychic phenomena. His name is Dr. Jeremiah Nixon, and he said my...my friend's sudden ability to glimpse the future wasn't all that unusual."

"Oh."

"Because he...my friend...has no experience with these types of visions, he doesn't have a track record in deciphering the missing details. Dr. Nixon feels we have no choice but to play it very safely, assume the danger that was sensed is not a spider on the wall, or a mouse on the floor, that scares the wits out of you."

"Oh."

"I ran the whole confusing mess past my family, and they agreed with Dr. Nixon. The danger might be something dumb like a mouse, or it could be life-threatening. Because we don't know, we have to deal with the worst-case scenario.''

"Oh. Well, did Dr. Nixon have an explanation as to why your friend saw *me?* I mean, he said it was reasonable that your buddy's psychic powers jigged instead of jagged, but why the visions of *me?''*

"There are a couple of theories." *Destiny.* "There's no sense wasting our time discussing them because they *are* only theories." *Soul mates.* "There aren't any hard, fast, concrete rules about this sort of thing."

"Oh. Well, why don't we just destroy the shawl?" Nancy shrugged. "No shawl, no danger."

"No, bad plan. Destroying the shawl might cause heaven only knows what to happen."

"Oh."

Tux frowned. "Your side of this conversation is so stimulating, I hardly know where to put myself. Could you contribute a little more than 'oh'?"

"You told me, then asked, that I listen to you. I'm listening. My 'oh' is to let you know that you have my full attention. Don't be so picky."

"Yes, ma'am," he said, grinning. "I swear, Nancy, you're really something."

"Something awful?"

His smile faded. "Oh, no, not even close. You're something special, very special."

"Oh," she whispered, as her heart skipped a beat. "Thank you, Tux Bishop."

"You're welcome, Nancy Shatner."

They were there again; the now familiar crackling sensuality, the heightened awareness, the heat, the hot, burning heat, all spinning around them with invisible threads.

Tux straightened and leaned back in his chair, breaking the spell. Nancy blinked twice, then let out a pent-up breath.

"Nancy," Tux said, "what I'm about to say will probably

cause you to declare war. Before you go off on a rip, though, please stop and think, realize that the plan I'm proposing is the only logical way to handle this. Okay? Are you ready to hear it with an open mind?"

Nancy nodded.

"Good. I need to be with you and the blue shawl twenty-four hours a day. Until we see this through to its proper end, I'll be living with you."

Nancy's eyes widened and her mouth dropped open in shock.

Before she could speak, an ever so cheerful waitress appeared with their now forgotten dinners.

After what seemed like an eternity, Nancy finally spoke.

"What?" she said.

Tux's hands shot up, palms out. "Stay calm. It's really the only solution, Nancy. Think about it." He nodded and said soothingly, "Let's eat our dinners while they're hot. Don't talk, just eat, and think about it.

"You'll realize that my sticking close to you is the only way to handle this situation." He pointed to her plate. "Eat, okay? Your mind will function better if you have some protein in your system."

Nancy slowly shifted her wide-eyed gaze to her dinner, absently wondering how on earth the meal had gotten in front of her. She lifted her fork and took a small bite of the baked potato, not tasting it, nor the sweet butter and sour cream.

Tux Bishop, her brain hammered, had just said he was moving into her apartment, was going to be living with her so he could protect her.

That was absurd.

That was absolutely ridiculous.

If he thought she was going to consent to such an asinine idea, he was out of his mind.

She was rejecting his idiotic plan, thank you very much. She just had to figure out a way to handle this muddled mess.

Nancy frowned as she chewed and swallowed a bite of steak.

Blast. How could Tux protect her from the danger his friend had seen and sensed in the visions, if he wasn't with her to protect her from the danger his friend had seen and sensed in the visions?

Calm down, Nancy, she told herself. She was mentally babbling. There had to be a better solution than Tux's proposal, but for the life of her, she couldn't come up with what it was.

"Nancy?" Tux asked tentatively. "How's your dinner?" Lame, Bishop, very lame. The meal was the last thing on her mind, and he knew it. "No one will be aware that I'm staying with you, if you're worried about your reputation. I'll park my vehicle blocks away from Buttons and Beads, and walk back to your place. I'll sleep on the sofa at night, and hang out in the back room of the store during the day. With any luck we'll know what the danger is in a couple of days, deal with it, and that will be that. Neat and tidy."

Nancy sliced one hand through the air. "Cut. Hold it. Wait a minute." She leaned slightly toward Tux. "I have a very big question." She paused. "Why? Why are you doing all this? *You're* not the one who saw the visions.

"You're putting your own life on hold. Isn't that a bit above the code of friendship? Heavens, I don't even know the name of your friend who has caused this bizarre situation."

This was it, Tux thought. The duplicity had gone on long enough. He'd been dreading that moment when he'd have to tell Nancy the truth, then see her pull back, become wary of him. But he couldn't postpone this any longer. He just couldn't.

"Nancy, please try to understand that I..." Tux started, then stopped and shook his head. "Forget it. There's no chance in hell you'll understand." He sighed. "Okay, here goes. My friend's name is me. What I mean is, *I'm* the one with the psychic powers. *I* saw the visions, sensed the danger."

Nancy frowned. "You? Well, for Pete's sake, why all this baloney about 'my friend this, my friend that'?"

"Because I detest having these psychic abilities, and even more, I hate having to deal with people's reactions to me when it becomes known I have them."

Nancy narrowed her eyes. "Are you saying you decided how I would respond? You didn't give me the right to react the way I saw fit? You *controlled* me and the entire situation to suit *you?*"

Tux shifted uncomfortably on his chair. "That sounds rather harsh but…yeah, I guess you could say that. I couldn't deal with the thought of you putting distance between us. You said yourself that this whole thing was creepy."

"The *situation* was creepy. A stranger having visions of me being in danger is definitely creepy. But you had no right to preprogram how I would behave. No right at all. You should have stepped forward and asked me if I believe in psychic powers. My answer would have been yes."

"You're kidding."

"You're despicable," Nancy said, glaring at him. "How dare you take total control of a situation in which I have a major role."

A smile broke across Tux's face. "You accept my psychic abilities, accept *me* as I am?"

"Yes, of course, why wouldn't I?"

Tux stood, leaned across the table, dropped a quick kiss on Nancy's lips, then sank back onto his chair.

"Thank you," he said, his smile gone. "That means more to me than I can ever begin to tell you. Thank you very much. I apologize for selling you short. I've learned an important lesson about communication and, well…trust. Will you forgive me for screwing up so badly? Please?"

"Yes," Nancy said softly, "I forgive you. I understand what it's like to want to be accepted for who you really are." Oh, yes, she knew. She fought a constant battle with her mother, yearning to hear that Ruth Shatner finally realized that Nancy was a grown woman with her own hopes and dreams. "I forgive you, Tux."

"Thank you."

They gazed at each other, warmly, gently. And another brick in a foundation of trust and understanding was put firmly in place.

Tux tore his eyes from Nancy's and cleared his throat.

"Well," he said, "I'm glad all that is out in the open. Now, let's get back to the business of my moving in with you until this mess is settled."

"But..." Nancy sighed. "Are you certain that's necessary?"

"Definitely."

"Well, I guess I'll have to agree, because I can't think of another plan to take the place of yours." She paused. "My apartment is very small. We'll be falling all over each other. I have a set way of doing things, I value my freedom, independence and...I hate this."

Tux smiled. "That's *my* line."

"Well, I do."

"I'm not crazy about it, either." He shrugged. "We gotta do what we gotta do. We're mature adults, capable of handling living in cramped quarters by compromising, respecting each other's space. Like I said, hopefully this will be a done deal in a few days."

Nancy sighed again. "All right. I think perhaps this is one of those situations that will be an amusing story to tell all my friends in about five years. When do you plan on putting this plan of yours into operation?"

"Tonight?" Tux cleared his throat. "Tonight, definitely tonight. I have a gym bag in the trunk of the car packed with some of my things. I knew that someone of your intelligence would see the merit of this proposal, and I came prepared to commence immediately."

"Translated," Nancy said, "that means you figured you could con me into this and you're ready to roll."

Tux shrugged. "Whatever."

"Don't you have a business to run?"

"I've got it covered. I'll be wearing a beeper in case anyone at the office needs to contact me."

The waitress appeared at the table. "Would you care for some dessert this evening?"

Nancy looked down at her plate, amazed to see that she'd finished her dinner, and wondered absently how it had tasted.

"Just coffee, please," she replied.

"Make that two," Tux said.

"All right," the girl said. "My, that's a pretty shawl. It's such a lovely shade of blue."

"Thank you," Nancy said. The waitress hurried away. "I'll give you the shawl," she added. "I'll even pay you to take it."

Tux chuckled. "Cheer up. We've got everything under control."

"Oh, right," she said, rolling her eyes heavenward. "On top of everything else, I now have a man living in my apartment. That's just super-duper dandy. I suppose you'll be in your investigator cum government agent mode, and move in toting a gun."

Tux nodded.

"I was kidding!"

"Nancy, I have to be prepared for anything. We don't know how serious the danger I sensed and saw is, remember? Everyone I spoke with advised me to play it safe and assume the worst."

"Swell, just great. I've just found out that your friend doesn't really exist, and in the next breath I have a live-in bodyguard, just like in that popular movie. Too bad I can't sing like Whitney Houston."

Tux laughed. "Too bad I don't look like Kevin Costner, the heartthrob of women around the globe."

Heaven forbid, Nancy thought. She was in enough trouble as it was with the sexy Mr. Bishop about to take up residence in her home.

She really did hate this.

Her independence, her I'm-in-charge-of-myself existence, seemed to be slipping through her fingers like some of her tiniest, shiny beads.

Tux had said that everything was under control? Well, that included the control of her life, and she'd struggled so hard for her freedom.

Now? Outside forces were dictating exactly how she was to function twenty-four hours a day. She felt smothered, felt as though she were running in place, getting nowhere in her attempt to escape from icy tentacles that had a voice of command, were telling her what to do.

She'd like nothing better than to lift her chin, narrow her eyes, point her finger toward the door of Buttons and Beads, and order Tux to go and never come back.

But she couldn't do that, because she believed in psychic phenomena. Tux would have known that from the beginning if he'd only asked. The visions he had seen had to be taken seriously. Granted, the danger might be something silly, like a spider on the wall. But what if it wasn't? What if it was dark and sinister?

Nancy inwardly sighed.

Forget pointing her finger at the door and ordering Tux out of her store and her life forever. She was stuck with the situation as it stood *and* with Tux Bishop.

Tell Tux to get out of her life forever? her mind echoed. *Forever?* Never see him again? Never be kissed, touched, held in his strong arms? Well, yes, that's the way she wished it could be. Just…poof, Tux Bishop, be gone.

Right? That's what she wanted.

Right? Of course.

Right?

Oh, Nancy, shut up, she told herself. She was exhausted, had dealt with too much in too short of a time. She just wanted to go home and crawl into bed.

Bed?

Oh, good grief, Tux was going to be sleeping a handful of feet away from her minuscule bedroom. There he'd be in all his magnificent, masculine glory, stretched out on her faded, lumpy sofa.

So? she argued. She wasn't some sex maniac, who would jump his gorgeous bones because she couldn't hold herself in check.

And Tux? He was a trained professional, had no doubt protected many other women in the past, had viewed them as nothing more than an assignment, just as he considered her to be.

Well, she wasn't an assignment, darn it, she was a woman.

"I'm cracking up," Nancy said, pressing a fingertip to her forehead. "I am. I'm totally losing it. I need some sleep."

"I wondered why you'd suddenly become so quiet over there," Tux replied, smiling. "Now I know...you were having a nervous breakdown." His smile faded. "You've been hit with a lot all at once, Nancy. Sleep is exactly what's called for here." He signaled to the waitress for the bill. "Let's get you home and into bed."

Bed? he thought. Somehow, during the drive from the restaurant to Buttons and Beads, he had to put his years of training into effect. He knew how to detach himself emotionally from the people involved in an assignment, and just do his job.

The problem was that he'd never kissed, held, gone up in flames with wanting one of said people before the mechanics of the assignment began.

Well, okay, he'd muddied the clinical waters by kissing

Nancy. So, he'd forget he'd kissed her, forget the heat of desire that had rocketed throughout him, forget how sensational she'd felt nestled against his aroused body.

He'd handle this like a pro.

Even if it killed him.

Five

When Tux stopped at the cashier's counter in the lobby of the restaurant, Nancy told him she was going to scoot into the powder room.

What she was doing, she admitted to herself, as she headed for the appropriate door, was buying herself a few more minutes of time before she and Tux started toward her apartment.

She was surprisingly fine about the revelation that Tux was actually the one possessing psychic powers. Granted, he could have told her the truth sooner, but she *did* understand his heart-felt desire to be accepted for who he was as a man. She *had* forgiven him for the white lie about "his friend."

But she would linger for as long as possible in the powder room, with the hope she'd gain at least a modicum of calmness regarding Tux taking up residency with her.

Forget it, she thought, pushing open the door to the ladies' room. She was a wreck and would remain a wreck, no doubt about it.

Inside the prettily decorated area, Nancy heard someone talking, but realized a moment later that the attractive woman in front of the mirror was speaking to her own reflection as she applied mascara.

"He cancels dinner because some big shot is coming in from New York for a hush-hush meeting," the woman said. "The nerve of that man."

She tossed the mascara into her purse and removed a blush compact. With swift, angry strokes, she began to brush a rosy shade onto her cheeks.

"Then he has his bozo bring me to this dump to eat. That muscle-bound creep had the gall to tell me that his highness said I wasn't to wear the ring in public because it cost a fortune and I might lose it."

The woman caught sight of Nancy in the mirror and spun around to face her.

"Men are duds," the woman declared. "Don't you agree? Idiots. I despise men. All of them."

"Oh, well, I…" Nancy shrugged, then placed her tote purse on the counter next to the woman's open evening bag.

"I've had it," the woman fumed on, as Nancy began to wash her hands. "I've really had it with Jimmy the Jerk. I can't wear the ring because I might lose it? I'm not a child, by damn, I'm a woman."

The woman swung her arm with such force to replace the blush compact, that both her and Nancy's purses were flung onto the floor.

"Oh, look what I've done," the woman said. "I'm so sorry."

"No problem," Nancy said.

Both women bent down to retrieve their belongings that had scattered across the polished tile floor.

"It's time he learned he can't treat me this way," the

woman decided, jamming things into her purse. "I'll teach him. Yes. Surprise, surprise."

The pair stood at the same moment, and the woman smiled at Nancy.

"Enjoy, honey," the woman said. "You just won the lottery."

"Pardon me?" Nancy said, totally confused.

"Ta-ta," the woman said, then spun on her three-inch heels and marched from the room.

"Whatever," Nancy said.

She washed her hands again, dried each finger *very* slowly, then decided she'd better go meet Tux before he sent the marines in after her.

Her hiatus in the powder room, she knew, had not soothed her jangled nerves one iota.

In the parking lot, Tux met the gaze of the huge man who was holding the back door of a large car open for the woman from the powder room. The two men nodded slightly in acknowledgment of the other.

"Who is that?" Nancy whispered.

Tux chuckled. "An honest-to-goodness thug. We crossed stormy paths last year. I don't know who he's working for at the moment."

"That woman was very angry because..." Nancy began. "Oh, never mind."

"Your chariot, ma'am," Tux said, sweeping one arm in the direction of his car.

It seemed to Nancy that the drive back to Buttons and Beads was taking two years, give or take a month or so. Each time she envisioned Tux in her tiny apartment, he looked bigger, incredibly massive, filling the small expanse to overflowing.

How would she be able to walk across a room without bumping into him? Everywhere she turned, he'd be so...so *there*. She wouldn't be surprised if there wasn't even enough air left for her to breathe.

She didn't want Tux in her home.

The apartment was her safe haven, a place where she could just *be*. It was a handful of square feet that declared her freedom from anyone demanding an explanation for what she was doing at any given moment, or dictating what she should do next.

And if it wasn't bad enough that someone would be crowding her, threatening her independence, that *someone* was Tux Bishop: masculinity personified, blatantly male, sensuous, compelling, mesmerizing Tux.

"Would you prefer that I park the car several blocks away from the store, Nancy?" Tux asked, snapping her back to attention.

"No, that won't be necessary," she said, flipping one hand breezily in the air. "My little family on the block will be thrilled to think there's a man in my house. Your being there will spice up their lives."

What about Nancy's life? Tux wondered. How did *she* really feel about him taking up residence in her apartment, not as a bodyguard…as a man?

Forget it. What difference did it make? When it came to Nancy Shatner, *bodyguard* was his official title. She'd probably forgotten about those kisses they'd shared, anyway, or she'd chalked them up as unimportant, no big deal.

That was a depressing thought. Those kisses had been…

"You can park behind the store," Nancy told him, "but I can't vouch for the safety of a car like this one in my neighborhood."

"Good point. I'd prefer not to have my Blazer stripped and ripped, either. I'll see if Blue will loan me an old pickup truck from his ranch. He's got some really junky vehicles out there that he drives until they gasp their last and die."

Nancy nodded.

"I've been thinking about something, Nancy," he said. "I saw you *wearing* the blue shawl in my vision, but I don't believe we can count on you only being in danger while you have it on. My predictions of the future aren't exactly fine-tuned. We're going to assume that because you *own* the shawl, things have been put into motion."

"I'm too tired to debate the issue," she said, sighing. "Except…"

"Yes?" he prompted, glancing over at her.

"The shawl is too warm to be worn in June. Even as a finishing touch to an outfit, it's not the season for it. Did it ever occur to you that your vision took place in the wrong time frame?"

Tux frowned. "No, it *didn't* occur to me." He chuckled. "Well, we ought to have living together down pat if nothing happens to put you in danger before September or October."

"No, by then you'll be in traction from having slept on my lumpy sofa for months," she said, laughing.

"Grim."

"Tux, seriously, you can't stay at my apartment for heaven only knows how long. We have to have a time limit, a point where we say enough is enough, and conclude that your vision was scrambled, or whatever."

"I don't know about that," Tux said thoughtfully.

"It makes sense," Nancy elaborated, becoming animated. "It's like seeing a preview to a movie, then going to the theater to watch the film and realizing the outtakes had presented a distorted impression."

"Well…"

"Try this other theory on for size. Suppose I'm not facing danger in my future, but merely some kind of upset. You know, I mess up an order for beads, or I receive a particularly exasperating telephone call from my…" Her voice trailed off.

"From who? Who might call and upset you?"

"That's not important. The point is, Tux, that the vision could have been magnified, as well as scrambled."

"Mmm."

In his mind's eye, Tux saw Nancy reaching out her arms, pleading for help. He saw her pale face streaked with tears, and the fear in her expressive dark eyes.

A chill shuddered through him as the remembrance of the danger he'd sensed on all three nights swept over him in crystal clarity.

"No," he said gruffly. "It's more than being upset because you messed up an order for beads. Yeah, maybe it's a mouse, a spider, but it's definitely something that frightens you very much. It's *not* an annoying incident like a telephone call that frustrated you."

"I'm not afraid of mice," Nancy said, folding her arms beneath her breasts. He'd burst her enthusiasm for the new theory like a balloon.

"Fine. Cancel the mouse."

"You don't have to be grumpy about it. My theory is reasonable, and you're dismissing it very quickly, if you ask me. Not that you're asking me. You're getting rather pushy again, Mr. Bishop. You're not running this show, snapping out orders that I'm supposed to say 'Yes, sir' to. We're in this together, equal partners. I have a voice and I *will* be heard."

"Why are you yelling?"

"Because it's the only way I can at least be halfway certain that you're listening to me."

"Hey, I've listened to everything you've said," he hollered.

"And you're set on automatic reject, as far as my ideas, my theories, are concerned. You are *not* totally in charge here, mister."

"I *know* that."

"Then act like it!"

"Hell," Tux muttered.

He whipped into the alley edging the row of stores and

parked behind Buttons and Beads. Nancy unsnapped her seat belt as Tux shut off the ignition, then she reached for the handle of the door. A yellow light bulb above the rear entrance to the store cast a dim glow over the interior of the car.

"Nancy, wait," Tux said quietly, as he released his seat belt. "Please."

She turned her head to glare at him, but maintained her grip on the door.

"I don't want to argue with you," he implored, looking directly at her. "Actually, this isn't an argument at all, in my opinion. It's a reaction to a helluva lot of stress. We *are* in this together, Nancy, just like you said. Together."

He leaned across the center console and cradled one of her cheeks with his hand, gently stroking the velvety soft skin with his callused thumb.

It was too much, it really was, Nancy thought. His gentle touch was the last straw, the one-too-many in a child's tower of blocks that caused it to crumble.

The combination of the funny flutter of heat that had swept through her when Tux had said "together" in that deep, rumbly voice of his, added to the soothing, yet sensuous, gesture of his large hand on her cheek, was tipping her over the emotional edge she was teetering on.

Two tears slid down her cheeks, followed quickly by two more.

"Oh, man," Tux said, "now I've done it."

He got out of the car, locked the door and sprinted around to Nancy's side. He assisted her from the vehicle, reached back in to grab the shawl, then locked the door behind her.

Nancy sniffled.

Tux encircled her shoulders with one arm and led her toward the rear of Buttons and Beads.

"Key?" he said.

She nodded, fished the key out of her purse and dropped it into his outstretched hand.

Stop crying, she told herself. Why was she crying? She didn't *know* why she was crying. She felt like crying, so she was.

How was she supposed to get Tux to treat her as an equal partner in this mess if she was crying like a kid? Oh, who cared? She was exhausted, and she'd cry until next Thursday if she wanted to.

"Oh-h-h, for Pete's sake," she wailed, "tell me not to cry. *Order* me not to cry. Demand that I stop crying right this instant."

Tux chuckled as he unlocked the door.

"Not me, babe. I've already had my head on a platter for giving orders. If crying makes you feel better, then go for it."

"Forget it," she said. "I don't have the energy to cry anymore." She dashed the tears from her cheeks. "There. I'm finished with that nonsense."

"Whoa," Tux exclaimed, glancing at the sky. "Look at that, would you?"

"What am I looking at?" she asked, tipping her head back.

"The moon. I've checked out moons all around the globe. I realize there's only one moon up there, but I swear there is nothing to compare anywhere to a Texas moon. Tell me I'm nuts, but it's true."

"You looked at the moon while you were in the middle of a dangerous assignment for the government?"

"Yes. I found a minute to do that, no matter what I was involved in. My statement stands...a Texas moon is the best in the world."

"Oh," she said softly, still staring at the heavens. "You're full of surprises, Tux Bishop."

"Yeah, well, let's get inside."

In the rear area of the store, Tux double-checked the lock on the door, then followed Nancy up the narrow, rickety stairs leading to the upper level.

He'd handled that pretty well, he thought. Nancy didn't

have a clue as to how ripped up he'd been when he'd seen her tears. It had taken all the willpower he possessed not to lift her into his arms, hold her close, tell her that nothing was ever going to hurt her, because he was there to protect her.

Nancy's tears were his fault. He felt like a villain in a *very* bad movie. He'd brought this bizarre scenario into her life, upset her, frightened her, caused her to cry. Damn.

Inside Nancy's apartment, Tux gestured for her to stay by the door. He turned on lights as he moved through the small rooms, mentally cataloging the spick-and-span cleanliness, as well as the faded, worn furniture.

"All clear," he said, draping the blue shawl over the back of a chair. "I forgot to get my gym bag out of the trunk of the car. You go on to bed. I'll be back in a few minutes."

Nancy opened a door to reveal a tiny linen closet. She removed a pillow and a set of sheets, then crossed the room to place them on the sofa.

"It's too warm for a blanket," she said. "This sofa is really awfully lumpy. I slept on it when my mother came to visit."

"I'll live."

"I'm sorry I yelled at you, Tux," she said, turning to face him. "And I also apologize for crying. I just..." She threw up her hands. "I don't know."

"Hey, it's okay. We're under a lot of stress. I'd cry, too, but then I'd probably be expected to eat quiche, because I would have lost my macho image. I hate quiche."

Nancy smiled. "Thank you for being so understanding. I'll be fine in the morning, I promise. I just need a good night's sleep."

"You bet," he said, nodding. "I'll...um..." He jerked one thumb toward the door. "I'll just zip down and get my bag."

"Yes."

They didn't move. They were hardly breathing. They weren't capable of tearing their gaze away.

And the heat, oh, the burning, churning heat, was sweeping through them like brushfires out of control.

Tux took one step toward Nancy.

Nancy took one step toward Tux.

Then they stopped.

Tux spun around, went to the door, and left the apartment, closing the door behind him.

Nancy blinked and drew a wobbly breath.

She was not, she decided wearily, going to think about the now familiar whatever-it-was that had just held her and Tux fast.

Thinking about *anything* else tonight was taboo. No more thinking, not tonight.

She sighed, then headed for bed.

But before she crawled between the cool, beckoning sheets, she went to the window to gaze once more at the Texas moon.

Six

When Nancy stirred the next morning there was only one coherent thought in her foggy mind.

"Coffee," she mumbled, flipping back the sheet on the bed.

She left the bedroom, eyes at half-mast, wearing a faded pink T-shirt that just barely covered her lacy, red bikini panties. Shuffling into the kitchen, she made a pot of coffee by rote, then leaned back against the counter and closed her eyes.

Wondering absently what day of the week it was, she decided she really didn't give a rip.

"Coffee, coffee, coffee," she chanted, not opening her eyes. "My kingdom for a cup of coffee."

"Sold," Tux said, coming into the small room.

Nancy's eyes flew open, and she stared at Tux as though he were an alien creature dressed in jeans and a knit shirt who had just landed in her apartment.

"Short memory, sunshine," Tux said, smiling. "It's me, Tux, remember? I have survived a night on the lumpiest sofa ever manufactured by man. I'm rise-and-shine fine, except for the fact that every muscle in my body is crying for mercy.''

His gaze swept over her, and he ordered himself to totally ignore the heat that coiled instantly low in his body from the scrutiny.

''Nice outfit,'' he observed breezily. ''My, my, are those really lacy red panties I see peeking from beneath that shirt, Ms. Shatner? Ah, women's secrets are such a delight to discover.''

Nancy was jolted from her stupor so quickly it was as though she'd chugalugged an entire pot of caffeine-laden coffee.

''Oh,'' she gasped. A warm flush of embarrassment stained her cheeks. ''I forgot you were here.''

She gripped the sides of the bottom edge of the T-shirt and yanked them down, hoping to cover the panties while escaping from the kitchen. The thin material of the shirt was pulled taut over her breasts, clearly defining them.

''Bad move,'' Tux said, his gaze riveted on her lush breasts.

Nancy glanced down, yelped in horror, then folded her arms across her breasts. The hasty motion hiked the shirt up again to reveal several inches of the lacy red panties.

''That didn't cut it, either,'' Tux said, his eyes shifting lower. ''Don't get me wrong. I'm enjoying these maneuvers, but I think you're in real trouble there, Ms. Shatner.''

And he was going to pass out on his face, he thought, if she didn't go put some clothes on. His oh-so-glib routine was as phony as a three-dollar bill. He was hanging on by a thread, but had no intention of letting Nancy know he was going up in flames.

He was also guarding the secret of the half hour he'd spent pacing around his car the previous night after retrieving the gym bag.

To his self-disgust, it had taken that long for his blood to cool and his heartbeat to return to a normal tempo. The sizzling sexual tension between him and Nancy in her living room had turned him inside out.

"What are you going to try next, Nancy?" Tux asked, raising his eyebrows. "This is fascinating, I must say."

Nancy narrowed her eyes.

Tux Bishop should not have messed with her, she fumed, before she'd had her coffee.

Nancy-after-coffee would have already disappeared from the kitchen.

But Tux had pushed Nancy-before-coffee, and that was a *very* big mistake on his part.

The coffee pot gurgled, hissed, then was quiet.

"Ah, my coffee is ready," she said, managing to produce a reasonably sincere smile. "Isn't that nice? Would you care for a mug?"

Before Tux could reply, she turned and opened the cupboard door behind her. There were several cups on the first shelf, and two extra ones on the top shelf.

She slowly, *so slowly,* lifted both arms, hands extended, to reach for the higher mugs. The T-shirt inched upward, little by little.

"Oh-h-h, man," Tux said, dragging both hands down his face. In the next instant he chuckled. "Okay, okay, you win, I quit. I was acting like a macho jerk."

Nancy glared at him over her shoulder. "Indeed."

She dropped her arms, straightened the shirt over the panties, then grabbed a cup from the bottom shelf. After pouring the steaming coffee into the mug, she started out of the kitchen, stopping in the doorway.

"Rule one," she said, half turning toward Tux. "Do not speak to me, or even acknowledge my presence, until I've had my coffee. To do so will definitely put your life in jeopardy."

"Yes, ma'am," Tux said, grinning at her. "I understand completely, ma'am."

"I certainly hope so," she said, with an indignant little sniff.

She tossed her head, her wild tumble of dark hair flying in all directions, and completed her exit with as much panache as her scanty attire allowed.

Tux watched her go then, laughing softly, and shook his head as he poured himself some coffee. He leaned back against the counter, crossing his feet at the ankles, and took a sip of the hot drink.

Nancy was really something, he thought. She'd nailed him, pure and simple. Score one for Ms. Shatner. He suddenly remembered a birthday present he'd gotten from his parents when he was seven years old.

His mother had used the old gimmick of wrapping a dozen boxes, each one bigger than the other, the diminishing in size packages hidden one inside the next.

The smallest box had produced the coveted treasure of a key to the lock on a new red bike that was stashed in the garage.

The memories of that present reminded him of Nancy: there were hidden treasures within her, waiting to be discovered, one at a time, a multitude of intriguing layers.

And the key to be found at her center, the innermost part of her? What would it open?

The door to her bedroom? No, that sounded like lust again, and his desire for Nancy was *not* just lust. He cared about her as a woman, a person.

Did the key belong to her heart?

Oh, no, he was dipping into the romantic mush. The key to her heart? How corny could a guy get, for crying out loud?

Forget the key. Forget the tower of mysterious packages, beckoning to be opened. *Forget Nancy Shatner.*

"The bathroom is free," Nancy said, whizzing back into the kitchen.

Forget Nancy? Tux's mind echoed. That was tough to do,

considering he was in the process of spending twenty-four hours a day with the lady. Oh, yeah, a really rough job, too, especially when she looked like she did now in jeans and a white blouse embroidered with a splash of colorful flowers.

The jeans were snug, accentuating her shapely legs and the feminine slope of her bottom. The blouse clung to the lush fullness of her breasts, which had been clearly defined earlier when she'd tugged the thin T-shirt taut.

Her hair was shiny, the wild waves fetching in their gypsy-like tumble.

Yes, Nancy was incredibly beautiful.

Forgetting her was totally impossible.

So forget *forgetting*. He'd concentrate on *remembering* that she was an assignment. Nothing more, nothing less. Just an assignment.

"You look very nice," he said quietly. "That's a pretty blouse."

"Thank you," she said, not looking at him. "I don't eat breakfast, but you're welcome to fix yourself something if you want to."

"I'll go shower and shave first." His gaze swept over her. "You're wearing a lot of colors there. Which one represents today, Thursday?"

She met his gaze. "Orange."

"And does orange Thursday have a significant something that it's known for?"

"It's the day of intuition."

Tux set his mug in the sink. "Intuition, huh? Interesting. I'll be sure and listen for my little voice, since it's having a high-profile day."

He left the kitchen, and Nancy refilled her mug.

Intuition, she mentally repeated. *Orange and intuition.* There was plenty of orange in her blouse, but how was her supply of intuition?

Was it telling her to put as much distance as possible between herself and Tux Bishop? If so, that was impossible. She was living with the man.

She laughed softly as she sat down at the small table by the window.

Her performance of wiggling her panty-clad bottom at Tux had been completely out of character. If she dwelled on it for too long, she'd probably go through the day with blushing pink cheeks.

In the distance she could hear the water in the shower start. That ordinary sound was one that millions of people took for granted every morning, she mused. Their partner in life was taking a shower.

But to her? It was such a foreign noise, that it might as well have been a roaring waterfall. There was a man in her apartment taking his morning shower, just as normal as you please.

Nancy drained the mug, set it aside, then propped one elbow on the table, her chin on the palm of her hand.

She sighed as she concentrated on the sound of the water.

There it was again, she realized, that chill of loneliness, an emptiness that had the ability to be heavy, pushing her down, down, with its oppressive weight.

It wasn't because the shower was running, she knew, it was due to the fact that in the days, weeks, months…dear heaven, *years*…after Tux was gone, she would hear no sounds—only taunting silence.

"Stop it, Nancy," she told herself.

She got to her feet, grabbed the mug and stomped to the sink. Her hand stilled as she stared at Tux's mug already there.

The water in the shower stopped, and she glanced over to the kitchen doorway. Then slowly and very carefully, she placed her mug next to Tux's in the bottom of the chipped sink. She nestled them close together, handles perfectly aligned.

After looking at her handiwork for a long moment, she spun around and left the room, mentally calling herself an idiot as she went.

* * *

The day passed quickly, due to the fact that the bell over the door of Buttons and Beads tinkled far more than usual.

Glenna had popped in the moment that Nancy had unlocked the front door of the store.

There was, Glenna announced, feigning innocence, a snazzy car in the alley behind Buttons and Beads. It had, in fact, been there *all night.* Did Nancy think they should call the police in case the vehicle had been stolen, then abandoned there?

Nancy had rolled her eyes heavenward at Glenna's charade, reintroduced Tux, then the parade of shop owners from the block began, everyone eager to meet the handsome man who had spent the night, and was now apparently staying the day, with their darling Nancy.

Tux took it all in stride, oozing charm, and Nancy finally relaxed and waited for the next nosy, albeit loving, neighbor to arrive.

Between visits, Tux helped Nancy count beads, quickly discovering he couldn't do two, four, six and talk at the same time.

In the late afternoon Tux telephoned Blue, then hung up the receiver and turned to look at Nancy.

"Blue has a truck I can borrow," he said. "He's so willing to be helpful, it worries me. I have a feeling he's going to put my car through its paces while he has it."

Nancy smiled, then sealed a bag of beads.

"We could grab a hamburger after you close the store, then drive out to Blue's ranch. Okay?"

"That sounds fine. I've never seen an authentic Texas ranch."

Tux sat back down across from her at the table and tipped the chair back onto two legs, folding his arms across his chest.

"You moved from Florida to Texas?" he said. "Why Texas?"

Nancy looked up at him quickly, then averted her eyes. She

busied herself checking off an item on the order blank, then reached for the frosting spatula again.

"Nancy? Why Texas?" Tux repeated.

She sighed and met his gaze.

"It was symbolic," she said. "I had an image in my mind of Texas being big and open, and gloriously free from restraints, just sprawled in all directions as far as the eye could see."

Tux nodded. "That's Texas. Why the need for the freedom from restraints?"

"It was time," she said. "Overdue, in fact." She lifted her chin. "I was determined to be independent, to take care of myself, to be accountable only to me. No one else. Not ever again."

Tux thudded the chair onto all four legs and rested his arms on the table.

"Who were you running from?" he asked, looking directly at her. "A lover?"

"It's none of your business."

"You're right, it's not. Now that we've agreed on that, answer the question."

"You're so pushy," she said, glaring at him.

He grinned. "Yeah, I know, but I'm cute. Who were you running from?"

"I wasn't running *from*," she said, her voice rising. "I was running *to*...my life, my future. *Mine*."

"Go on," he urged.

Nancy studied Tux for a long moment, a thoughtful expression on her face.

"I haven't told anyone on the block why I moved here," she said quietly. "I was afraid it would sound childish. But...well, you weren't open with me at first about your having psychic powers, because you were convinced I'd stand in judgment of you."

"I was wrong," Tux said, watching her face intently.

"Yes, you were. You could have trusted me, *in* me, much sooner than you did, and I was angry, hurt in a way, because you didn't. So, fair is fair. I'm going to tell you *now* why I came here from Florida. I'm trusting in you to not stand in judgment of *me*, Tux."

A strange tightness gripped Tux's throat, and his heart thundered in his chest. He had a sudden image in his mind of pretty paper floating away from a box in a tower of boxes, that beckoned to him to discover the treasure within.

That was what Nancy was doing at that very moment...giving him the gift of trust. It was one more layer, one more part of the intriguing woman that was Nancy Shatner.

"Thank you, Nancy," he said, his voice raspy.

She smiled at him warmly, then her smile faded, shifting into a frown.

"It's not a soap opera quality story, Tux. There was no lover dominating me in Florida. It's a simple, boring case of a child born late in life to parents who then expected the child to be their companion for life.

"My mother has gotten worse, more clinging, dependent, since my father died. I couldn't breathe anymore. I had to be...*have* to be free. I was afraid I'd sound like a little girl running away from her mommy if I tried to explain it to Glenna and the others."

"I see," Tux said slowly. "I understand, I really do, and you certainly aren't being childish. You deserve a lot of credit, respect, for coming here on your own, starting a business, the whole nine yards." He paused. "But you don't have to be totally alone to be free, Nancy."

She got to her feet and picked up the bin of beads.

"*I* do," she said.

"Why?"

"Because my freedom was hard-won, and I'm very protective of it. I never intend to allow anyone to *own* a part of me again…not my mother, a lover, a husband. My stand on the issue is etched in stone.''

Tux frowned as he watched Nancy leave the rear area of the store.

That lady has an attitude, he thought. A lover, husband, wouldn't *own* her, require her to give a part of herself away. That wasn't how it worked, not by a long shot. Nancy was sentencing herself to a lonely existence for no reason.

That wasn't good at all. He was going to work at broadening her narrow-minded attitude. Love, marriage, *added* to a person's life, it didn't take away. Yeah, he'd just have to straighten Ms. Shatner out on the subject.

Why?

Tux's frown deepened.

Why? He didn't know why he was now determined to shift Nancy's way of thinking.

Maybe it was because… Well, sure, that was it. Counting beads by two, four, six was boring as hell. Since he was stuck here until the mystery of the danger surrounding the blue shawl was solved, fixing Nancy's attitude would be a challenge beyond bead counting.

Yes, it had meant a lot to him that Nancy had trusted him with one of her innermost secrets, but her attitude had nothing to do with him personally. Working on Nancy's mind-set was simply a means by which to help pass the time. It would add a little spice to protecting Nancy from danger.

Nancy, who was his temporary assignment, nothing more.

Yes, Tux thought, getting to his feet, it sure felt great knowing he was once more in control of himself and in charge.

Everything was going just fine.

Seven

After stopping at a fast-food restaurant for a quick dinner, Tux and Nancy headed for Blue's ranch, the shawl tossed into the narrow back seat of the car.

They chatted easily, one topic flowing into the next. Tux drummed his fingers on the steering wheel to the rhythm of a peppy country-and-western song on the radio.

"You know," he said, glancing over at Nancy, then back to the road, "I was impressed with all those orders I saw at Buttons and Beads today. You've got an excellent cross section of customers."

Nancy nodded. "Yes, I'm very pleased. The large order from the school district for the art departments was a real coup."

"The one from the activity director at the nursing home wasn't bad, either. Then there were all those requests from individuals. You're on a roll, Ms. Shatner."

Nancy laughed. "Cross your fingers that things keep on

rolling. I've negotiated with a distributor and I'm going to start offering a selection of kits. A person would have everything they needed to make a beaded purse, or belt, or whatever, with instructions included.''

"Dynamite." Tux paused. "Yes, ma'am, you're a savvy businesswoman.''

"Well, thank you, sir," she said, smiling. "I... Oh, look Tux, there's a sign by the side of the road advertising an estate sale up ahead. Could we stop? Please?''

"Sure," he said, reducing his speed. He frowned. "Why?''

"Because this is ranch country. Some of these homes have been lived in by the same family for generations. There might be some marvelous old beads or buttons there.''

"Oh." He shrugged. "Okay, we'll stop. Blue's ranch is the one beyond this place. He has probably been over here buying up all the good stuff.''

"I see estate sales advertised in the newspaper, but most of them are too far off the bus line for me to get to. Oh, this is so exciting.''

Tux chuckled. "If you say so.''

"I say so. There...up ahead beyond that tree is a sign with an arrow. Turn right.''

"Got it.''

Tux left the main road and immediately slowed his speed to a near-crawl as he encountered a dirt road that had a generous supply of potholes.

Nancy leaned as far forward as her seat belt would allow, looking at the two-story house in the distance.

Tux smiled as he maneuvered the low-slung vehicle around the deepest ruts.

Man, oh, man, he thought, Nancy was making him feel about ten feet tall. Her dark eyes were sparkling with anticipation and pure joy. *He* had made Nancy happy and, Lord, it felt good.

All he'd done was agree to a simple request to take her to an estate sale, and he felt like a hero, a knight in shining armor. He'd never met anyone like Nancy Shatner, that was for sure. She was so…real. Yeah, that was a good word: *real.*

She was honest and open, probably had no idea how to play the game, didn't know the rules of the singles scene.

She was just Nancy.

And he liked her…a lot.

Tux parked the car next to a pickup truck that was in a row of trucks, his sports car definitely looking out of place.

The ranch house was obviously ancient and needed a coat of paint. The scrub grass front yard was strewn with various garden tools on one side, and a stretch of cluttered tables on the other. A sign on the front door of the house delivered the message Do Not Enter.

"Looks like this is an outside deal," Tux said, as they walked toward the house.

"Well, there's no telling how long it has been going on," Nancy said. "The furniture and such may have been sold days ago. I think we might be getting in on the odds and ends of what's left over."

"Well, enjoy," Tux said. "Don't rush. We're in no big hurry to get to Blue's."

She smiled up at him. "Thank you, Tux. This is such fun."

He matched her smile, then slid one arm across her shoulders as they approached the tables. Slowly and reluctantly, he dropped his arm back to his side to allow Nancy to move closer to the table, where several women were already browsing.

As Nancy began to examine the treasures on display, Tux swept his gaze over the men poking through the equipment on the other side of the yard.

It was an automatic gesture on his part, born of his many years as an agent. He wanted to know who was close to him and why they were there.

He mentally cataloged the jeans-clad men as ranchers, then his attention was caught by the tinny-sounding beep of the pager clipped to his belt. He pressed a button on the device, then watched a number march across the minuscule screen.

His office telephone number, he thought. Fine. He'd call in when they arrived at Blue's.

Tux relaxed and waited for Nancy, enjoying the peacefulness of being out of the hustle and bustle of the city. A short time later, Nancy hurried toward him.

"Tux," she said, coming to where he stood. "Look at this. Oh, this is so great."

Tux stared at a dusty, quart-size lidded jar that Nancy was holding up for his inspection.

"Great?" he said. "You like dirty bottles?"

"No," she said, laughing. She lifted the jar higher for his scrutiny. "It's full of buttons. See? This is exactly what I was hoping to find. It only cost two dollars, and I'm going to have such fun sorting through all these buttons. Who knows how many generations ago this became the official button jar of the house."

"Which only goes to show you."

"Show me what?"

"That this really is an orange intuition day," he said, smiling at her. "Your intuition said we should stop here and…bingo…you've got a grungy jar that's older than dirt. What a deal."

Nancy laughed. "This is obviously not your thing, as they say. Well, fine, I'm thrilled enough for both of us. Thank you for bringing me here."

Tux dropped a quick kiss onto her lips. "You're welcome."

They continued to smile at each other, sharing the moment. For that instant they were ordinary people, having done an ordinary thing like stopping to browse at a yard sale. They were having fun together, and it felt wonderful.

Back in Tux's car, Nancy took a tissue from her purse and

dusted off the jar. Holding it up to eye level, she began to turn it slowly in her hands, smiling in delight.

"Oh, look at that one," she said. "There's another lovely one, and another. What a marvelous treasure."

Tux chuckled as he left the dirt path and returned to the main road.

"Well," he said, "I sure know what you'll be doing when we get home tonight. You'll have those babies spread out on the kitchen table."

Nancy looked over at him quickly, then redirected her attention to the jar, no longer seeing the intriguing variety of buttons.

When we get home tonight, her mind echoed. There was no denying that a strange warm flutter had tiptoed around her heart when Tux had said those words. *When we get home tonight.*

Nancy cradled the bottle in both hands, rested them in her lap, and looked out the side window.

She was reacting…no, *over*reacting…to a simple statement that didn't even mean what it would sound like to a stranger. She and Tux wouldn't "get home tonight" in the normal sense. They had been thrown together under the same roof by circumstances beyond their control.

She *knew* that, darn it, yet she'd still registered a lovely sense of belonging, of togetherness, when Tux had said what he had.

Oh, she was being so foolish. She didn't even *want* a togetherness type relationship in her life. She *had* to be free, could not, would not, turn a portion of herself over to another person's control.

Tux was confusing her, muddling her brain. It was all his fault, the sexy, rotten rat.

And now she sounded about four years old. Enough of this.

"What's the name of Blue's ranch?" she asked, pulling herself from her jumbled thoughts.

"The Rocking B. He has owned his place for about ten years now. He's really shaped it up, has it operating in the black. He runs cattle, plus a few horses. Bram owns a construction company that's doing very well, too."

"And none of you are married?"

We're working on it, Tux thought dryly, *and failing miserably so far.*

"No," he said. "Our mother is painting pictures for baby nurseries, but..." He shrugged. "One of these days she'll have some grandkids."

The next few minutes passed in comfortable silence, then Tux slowed his speed.

"The Rocking B, ma'am," he announced.

Tux drove beneath an iron archway with the name of the ranch in scrollwork across the top. Nancy sat up straighter to get a better view.

She could see a two-story, pale blue house, pristine white corral fences, several other buildings of varying sizes that were painted brown, and an enormous red barn. In the distance were a multitude of grazing cattle.

"A real Texas ranch," she said, smiling. "It's perfect. It looks exactly the way I imagined a Texas ranch would."

"Well, good. I'm glad you like it," Tux said, laughing. "I'll tell Blue he can keep it."

"Definitely. It has my stamp of approval."

Tux drove to the front of the home and turned off the ignition. Before he could get around to assist Nancy from the vehicle, Blue emerged from the house.

"Hey, Tux," Blue yelled, smiling, "park that hunk of garbage out of sight, will ya? You're making my spread look tacky."

"Suffer," Tux said, matching his brother's smile.

Tux opened Nancy's door, but as he moved around it with the intention of extending his hand to her, Blue beat him to it.

"You must be Incredibly Beautiful Nancy," Blue said. "I'm Blue Bishop."

Nancy laughed. "That's a lovely title you gave me, but I'm just Nancy Shatner." She set the jar of buttons on the floor of the car, then got out of the vehicle, extending her hand to Blue. "I'm pleased to meet you."

Blue shoved his Stetson up with his thumb, then shook Nancy's hand.

"The pleasure is all mine," he said. "That title was the one Tux gave you when he told us about you. He got it right, I'll give him that. A person could probably count on one hand the number of things Tux has done right in his life, but he's on the mark this time."

"Speaking of hands," Tux said, frowning. "Could Nancy have hers back now?"

"Oh, sure," Blue said, releasing it. "I wasn't going to keep it, I was just enjoying it."

"Mmm." Tux glared at him.

It was impossible, Nancy thought, not to smile at the nonsensical banter between the brothers. And to think there was another brother besides these two. Their poor parents. They must have been in a constant state of exhaustion while raising the boys.

Blue was handsome, she mused, his features rugged and tan. He and Tux looked very much alike, yet with enough differences to make each unique.

"Want something cool to drink?" Blue said, looking at Nancy, then Tux.

"Sounds good," Tux said, nodding.

"Hey, did you bring the blue shawl?" Blue said. "I want to see that spooky thing."

Tux moved around and retrieved the shawl from the back seat.

Blue held up both hands. "I don't want to touch it, I just wanted to look at it. It's a blue shawl, all right. Weird."

Tux tossed the shawl onto the front seat, then closed the car door. The three went inside the house, where Nancy complimented Blue on the living room. It was decorated in big, heavy furniture that definitely announced that a man resided there.

"I need to use your phone, Blue," Tux said. "I had a message on my pager to call my office and—"

Before Tux could finish his sentence, the pager beeped again. Tux frowned when he saw the number displayed.

"Bram," he told them. "He must have just gotten home from the construction site."

"You make your calls," Blue said, "and I'll get us something to drink. Nancy, don't tell our mother that we left a guest alone two minutes after you arrived. She'd have a fit."

Nancy laughed. "Your secret is safe with me."

Blue rattled off what he had to offer to drink, then he and Tux left the room. Nancy sat down on a marshmallow-soft sofa. Blue soon returned with a glass of lemonade for Nancy and cans of beer for himself and Tux. Tux reappeared moments later.

Blue settled onto an enormous chair and Tux sat next to Nancy on the sofa. Nancy smiled as she watched the brothers prop ankles on opposite knees at exactly the same time.

"Well," Tux said, dragging one hand through his hair, "something is cooking, but I sure as hell don't know what it is."

"Yeah?" Blue said.

Nancy looked at Tux questioningly.

"Nancy," Tux continued, "do you remember that big guy we saw at the restaurant last night? The one I said was an authentic thug?"

Nancy nodded. "Yes."

"His name is Butch something-or-other. He was hooked up with some sleazy people last year when I tangled with him. His bosses landed in jail, but there wasn't any hard evidence against Butch. I have no idea who he's working for now."

"So what's with him?" Blue asked.

"He came by my office looking for me," Tux said. "When he came up dry there, he went to Bram's and asked him where I was. He was leaning against Bram's front door when our brother got home."

"Why on earth does he want to see you?" Nancy said.

Tux shrugged. "Beats me. He was polite at the office and at Bram's, asked if I was there, then did they know where I was. He said he needed to talk to me right away."

"Did he leave a message saying how you could reach him?" Blue said.

"Nope. He said *he'd* find *me*. His type are not real quick to give out their addresses." Tux paused. "All I can do is wait until he contacts me for whatever reason. If it wasn't for this situation with Nancy, I'd not think another thing about Butch."

Blue shook his head. "Man, you are sure knee-deep in your…your friend's psychic power, Tux."

"I told Nancy the truth, Blue," Tux said. "She knows I'm the one with the powers."

"Oh?" Blue smiled at Nancy. "See how special you are, Incredibly Beautiful Nancy? Tux would rather eat worms than spill the beans about his psychic abilities."

Nancy turned to look at Tux, smiling at him warmly. Their gazes met, held, and heartbeats began to quicken.

Blue cleared his throat.

Both Nancy and Tux jerked, then looked at Blue.

"Hi," Blue said, grinning. "Remember me? I live here. Hey, Tux, did you see the estate sale signs for The Bar None when you drove by? It's being auctioned off for back taxes. I hope I get some new neighbors who will shape up the place. That's good ranch land over there."

"We stopped at the estate sale so Nancy could look at the junk," Tux said.

"My button jar is *not* junk," she said.

"Sorry, ma'am," Tux said, chuckling.

"Dump that jerk, Nancy," Blue said. "Do you want to marry me?"

"No thank you," she said pleasantly. "It was nice of you to ask, though."

"It was worth a try," Blue said. "You really *are* incredibly beautiful."

"Would you knock it off?" Tux interjected, but Blue ignored him.

"So, Nancy," Blue said, "you got a jar of buttons at The Bar None, huh?"

"Yes, I did, and I'm eager to look at them all. There could be some real treasures in that bottle, especially if that ranch has belonged to the same family for several generations."

"It has," Blue said. "A Taylor has been on that land since the 1800s, I think. The last Taylor died a few months ago, though. Say, Nancy, there's a litter of new kittens in the barn. Would you like to see them?"

"Oh, yes, that would be fun."

"Can you make it to the barn, Tux?" Blue cajoled. "Or would you rather rest, wait here for us?"

Tux got to his feet. "You're not cute, Blue. Where in the hell did you ever get the idea that you were cute?"

"Our mother told me I was. Nancy, don't you think I'm cute?"

"You're adorable," she said, laughing.

"Hot damn," Blue said. "I'm telling you, Tux, offer to show a woman newborn kittens, and she's putty in your hands. Incredibly Beautiful Nancy is all mine."

"Wrong," Tux asserted, slipping his arm across Nancy's shoulders. "This lady is *mine.* Lead the way to the kittens."

"Let's go out the front door," Blue said, "due to the fact that the kitchen could use some tender lovin' care, like loading the dishwasher and sweeping the floor. I really need a wife."

"You need a maid," Nancy said.

"Her, too," Blue said. "Our mom said we're not to expect a wife to be the cleanup person."

"I think I'd like your mother," Nancy said.

"She'd like you, too. I bet she'd enjoy seeing all those buttons you got at The Bar None. Don't you think so, Tux?"

Tux nodded as the trio started toward the door, Tux's arm still firmly around Nancy's shoulders.

"Yeah, I imagine Mom *would* like to see the buttons," Tux agreed. "Maybe I'll take Nancy and the junky jar over there one of these nights."

"It's not…" Nancy started to say.

"Sorry," Tux said, laughing. "It's not a junky jar. It's a wonderful jar, a fantastic jar."

"Say now, Nancy," Blue said, opening the front door, "if you won't marry me, will you marry brother Bram?"

"I can't," she said. "I'm very busy at my store these days."

"Oh," Blue said, as they went outside. "Well, so much for that. I guess you'll just have to marry Tux, since he's camping at your store where you're so busy, anyway. That would be very efficient."

"I'll give it some thought." Nancy burst into laughter. "You guys are totally bonkers."

Blue went on and on about the fact that he was perfectly sane, but that Tux and Bram had lost it years ago, the poor devils.

As they headed toward the barn, Tux felt a prickly sensation on the back of his neck.

Why, he asked himself, did Hood-for-Hire Butch want to talk to him?

What in the hell was going on?

Even more, did it have anything to do with the danger he'd sensed threatening Nancy?

Eight

In the barn, Blue showed Nancy where the kittens were playing in a stall strewn with fresh hay. She sank to her knees next to the little creatures, then looked over at Tux where he stood about ten feet away.

"Tux?" Nancy said. "Aren't you going to come see these darlings?"

"Nope," he said. "The last time I played with kittens out here, one of them bit me. Those little guys are mean."

"Oh, for Pete's sake," she said, laughing.

"Listen," Tux stated, "you enjoy those furry mice, and Blue and I will go get squared away on the vehicle I'm going to borrow."

Nancy picked up one of the kittens. "Okay. I'll stay right here." She lifted the kitten to eye level. "Hello, hello. Aren't you the cutest thing?"

"Don't say I didn't warn you if it bites your nose," Tux

warned. "Come on, Blue, let's see the fine vehicle I'm to have the honor of driving around Houston."

The brothers left the barn and headed toward the back of the building.

"She's a winner, Tux," Blue said. "I really like your Nancy."

"She's not mine," Tux said gruffly.

"Why not? Hey, you must think she's special because you told her about your psychic abilities. She seems to be accepting that news flash just fine. Tell me one thing that's wrong with her that would eliminate her as a candidate for your wife."

"I didn't choose her."

Blue stopped walking and frowned at Tux. "What?"

"Blue, Nancy was dropped into my life by forces beyond my control." He stopped and looked at his brother. "I'm also staying close to her twenty-four hours a day because of circumstances beyond my control."

"So?"

"So Tux Bishop," he said, thumping himself on the chest, "picks his own woman. I won't be dictated to by psychic powers." He started walking again.

Blue fell in step beside him. "You're certifiably nuts, big brother. Nancy really is incredibly beautiful, just like you said she was. She's got a good sense of humor. She's intelligent, and she has maternal instincts because if she didn't, she wouldn't give a rip about newborn kittens.

"Hell, Tux, I'm not saying you should marry her tomorrow, but I sure do think she'd make a wonderful wife. You should at least discover what you two might have going together."

"No."

"Because you don't like the way she happened to enter your life? You're hung up on some ridiculous macho trip. Hell, I wouldn't care if a woman like Nancy was delivered to me by

UPS, just as long as she arrived on my doorstep. You're a weird biscuit, Bishop.''

"Shut up, Blue. The subject is closed.''

"Fine," he said, pulling his Stetson low on his forehead. "I heard you loud and clear. You don't want Nancy. Okay, then I'm going to ask her out to dinner.''

Tux's hand shot out to grip Blue's biceps. "The hell you are.''

Blue shrugged. "Why not? *I* think she's possible wife material.''

"You're not taking Nancy out, Blue!''

"I repeat…why not?''

Tux dropped his hand and dragged his fingers though his hair in a restless gesture.

"Because…yeah, because *I* have to be with her all the time to protect her from whatever danger is connected to the blue shawl. I'm not saying you can't take care of yourself, or a woman who might be with you, Blue, but this is *my* problem and I intend to see it through to its proper end.''

Tux nodded decisively.

"So there you have it," he concluded. "You can't go out on a date with Nancy. Facts are facts.''

"Right." Blue coughed to cover up a burst of laughter. "I understand perfectly.''

"Good." Tux glared at his brother, then strode ahead of him.

Blue followed slowly behind, grinning. "Tux, you idiot," he muttered under his breath, so his brother wouldn't hear him, "Incredibly Beautiful Nancy has gotcha, and I sure as hell hope you figure that out before you lose her, lamebrain.''

Still chuckling softly, Blue caught up with Tux behind the barn, where a pickup truck was parked. The vehicle had very little paint remaining on the dull gray exterior, the few splashes of color being pea-soup green, mustard yellow, and muddy brown.

"What is it?" Tux asked, staring at the truck. "Even more, what happened to it?"

"Hey, that truck is in its prime. It has just been broken in. It'll get you where you need to go, and I doubt seriously that anyone will try to rip it off."

"You've got that straight," Tux said, smiling. "Even a thief wouldn't want to be seen in that thing." He paused, his smile disappearing. "Blue, I need to talk to you alone. That's why I left Nancy in the barn with the kittens."

"Okay. What's up?"

"Maybe something, maybe nothing, but under the circumstances, the visions I saw, I can't take any chances. Butch is trying to locate me, and I don't know why. The thing is, he saw me with Nancy. It's probably no big deal, but I can't run the risk of ignoring the fact that Butch seems determined to track me down."

Blue nodded. "Makes sense to me. So, what's the plan?"

"I need some time to see if I can find out why Butch is looking for me. What I'd like to do is borrow a Stetson, which will make me look enough like you when I leave here in the truck.

"If Butch is watching your place, ready to tail me to corner me when I'm alone, for heaven only knows what reason, he'll think I'm still on the ranch because my car will be in plain view."

"The problem is," Blue said, "that Nancy will be in the truck with you. Butch might believe she's going somewhere with me, but what if *she's* the one he's interested in? Why a gun-toting hood would be concentrating on Nancy, I sure don't know. But..."

"Yeah, I see your point," Tux agreed, hooking one hand over the back of his neck. "I've got no choice but to scare Nancy by telling her she has to lie low and out of sight in the truck when we leave here."

Tux stopped talking and stared at his brother for a moment.

"You realize that if Butch believes that Nancy and I are still here and he runs out of patience waiting for us to leave, you're possibly being set up for a visit from him," Tux finally said to Blue. "He has been pleasant so far, but his mood might change at any minute."

"That's what shotguns are for," Blue said. "Don't worry about that part."

"Listen, if he shows up here, be cool, act cautious. He'll probably tell you why he wants to talk to me, or to Nancy. Pretend to buy it after a while, and tell him we're at Buttons and Beads. Okay?"

"Got it."

"This whole thing with Butch may be nothing, but someone, or something, is prepared to put Nancy in danger. I have to play out every hand that's dealt."

Blue nodded. "Yes."

Tux glanced at the sky. "It's getting dark. I want to head out of here while I can be seen behind the wheel of the truck, but not too clearly. I guess I'd better go ruin Nancy's day."

"Are you serious?" Nancy said, staring at Tux in the barn.

"Very serious," Tux said. "Nancy, look, I don't know if all this is necessary, but I can't take any chances. By making it appear that you and I stayed here, I'm buying some time to check out things regarding our buddy Butch."

Nancy wrapped her hands around her elbows. "Yes, I understand."

Tux placed one hand gently on her cheek. "Hey, hang in there, okay? I'm probably making a big deal out of nothing."

"I'm all right," she said, managing a smile. "I was having such a lovely time, I guess I just forgot that we're still involved in this mess." She shifted her gaze to Blue, and Tux dropped his hand from her face. "Thank you for letting me play with the kittens, Blue."

"Anytime," he said, smiling at her.

"All right," Tux said, "let's go. We'll walk up to the front of the house, get your purse, the shawl and the button jar out of the car, then go into the house.

"Blue, you drive the truck to the rear of the house. We'll put Nancy's things in the truck, you give me a Stetson, and we'll leave. Nancy, you'll have to hide until I'm certain we're not being followed."

"Oh, good grief," she muttered, rolling her eyes heavenward. "If I was watching this movie on television, I'd turn it off and go to bed."

"Well put," Blue said, chuckling. "I think it's a grade C flick."

"Look at the bright side," Tux said, grinning at Nancy. "You have a starring role."

"Yuck," she said, then started toward the barn door.

"Definitely a wife candidate," Blue whispered to Tux, then ducked.

As Nancy retrieved her belongings from Tux's car, she felt like a bug under a microscope, being watched by a huge, menacing eye.

This situation, she thought wearily, was getting out of hand very quickly. Everything had been kicked up a notch, flinging her into a frightening arena where she was lost and afraid. She didn't know the rules of how to survive.

That huge Butch person, who no doubt carried a gun, was possibly going to follow Tux? Or follow her? Or follow both of them?

It was too much, it really was, because it was too *real*. That creepy man was a living, breathing human being who might very well be intent on doing her harm.

But why?

Nancy stood by Tux's car, hugging the shawl, her purse and the button jar, frowning as she stared into space.

This did *not* make sense. Why on earth would a big-league

hood be interested in little-league, honest-citizen her? It was ridiculous, really absurd.

But no matter how many times she told herself that, it didn't cause the cold fist of fear in her stomach to melt, just disappear. It didn't remove her sense of vulnerability, of being controlled, dictated to by sources unknown.

She was running out of emotional room to put it all and was rapidly approaching overload.

"Nancy?" Tux called, from the front doorway. "Are you coming?"

"What?" she said, snapping her head around. "Oh, yes, of course."

Behind the house, Tux slid behind the wheel of the shabby truck, then settled a Stetson firmly on his head. Blue closed the door of the vehicle, then gave it a friendly pat.

"Don't underestimate this baby," Blue said. "One of my hands is really into tinkering under the hood of anything that has a motor to tinker with. This truck looks like hell, but it would give your sports car a run for its money in the straightaway."

"Not in this lifetime," Tux replied, "but at least there's hope we'll actually make it back into town in this bucket of bolts."

"Oh, ye of little faith," Blue chided, shaking his head. "You're such a pain in the butt."

Tux chuckled, then his smile changed to a frown as he looked over to see Nancy standing by the open door on the passenger side.

"Hey, you're white as a sheet," he said gently. "I'm sorry I've frightened you, Nancy. There probably isn't a thing to worry about. We'll zip into town with no problem, and you'll be at your place before you know it. Get in the truck. Okay?"

Nancy sighed. "Okay. I hope you're at least earning your secret decoder spy ring for choreographing this nonsense."

Blue hooted with laughter.

"I'll gladly settle for it turning out to be nonsense," Tux said.

Nancy wrapped the button jar in the shawl, then set it on the floor of the truck, tucking her purse next to the bundle. She climbed up onto the seat just as Blue arrived on her side to close the door behind her.

"Well, get as comfortable as you can," Tux said. "There's not a lot of room in here, but you're not very big. Fold, scrunch, whatever it takes to keep you below the view through the windows."

Nancy wiggled this way, then that. She wrapped her arms around her knees, then slowly toppled to the right, whacking her head on the door.

"Ow!" she yelled.

"Say 'damn it,'" Blue said. "It'll make it feel better."

"Ow, damn it!" She rubbed her head. "That didn't help one bit."

"Try the other direction," Blue said, through the open window.

That maneuver resulted in her head hitting the solid muscles in Tux's upper arm.

"Oh-h-h," she said, holding her head. "This isn't going to work."

"Sure it is," Blue said. "I see what the problem is, Nancy. There's just a tad more of you than there's seat to fit you in. So, pull up your knees again, but this time rest your head on Tux's thigh."

"What?" Nancy and Tux said in unison.

"Trust me," Blue said. "This will work. Hey, wait a minute." He opened the door, took out the button jar, and unwrapped the blue shawl. Putting the jar back on the floor, he braced it with Nancy's purse, then folded the shawl into a square. "There you go," he said, handing the shawl to Nancy. "A pillow."

Nancy stared at the shawl, Tux's thigh, then met Tux's gaze, matching his frown.

"I don't have a better idea," Tux told her. "Give it a try."

Nancy tentatively propped the shawl pillow on Tux's leg, then eased herself slowly down to rest her head on the blue square.

Blue closed the door. "Bingo. It works. You're still a pretzel, Nancy, but at least you're a pretzel that fits in the truck. It was nice meeting you, by the way. Keep me posted on all of this, Tux."

"Mmm," Tux rumbled, scowling as he turned the key in the ignition. The engine roared to life. "See ya, Blue."

Blue peered in the window. "Bye, Nancy."

"Bye, Blue," she said, with a weary sigh. "Thanks for your help."

Tux put the truck into gear and drove slowly from behind the house to the dirt stretch that would take them to the main road.

"It's getting dark real quick and there's a big, old Texas moon starting to shine like a silver ball. Fantastic," Tux said. "How are you doing down there?"

"Oh, fine," Nancy said, striving for a casual tone of voice. "Just great. No problem."

Her nose was going to grow, she thought, because her optimistic report was a bold-faced lie. She wasn't fine, she was dying!

She'd had no time to lecture herself on the fact that she could handle having her head nestled on Tux's thigh, she was just suddenly there...and dying.

Oh, heavenly days, his leg was so solid and strong, so incredibly masculine. Every time he moved from the gas pedal to the brake and back, she could feel the muscles bunch and shift.

Heat was thrumming low within her, growing hotter with every beat of her racing heart. No, she had not been prepared for this, and the result was a building desire that was threatening to consume her, send her up in a flash of passionate flames.

This was, she thought dismally, going to be a *very* long ride into town.

Tux's jaw was clenched so tightly that his teeth ached and his grip on the steering wheel had turned his knuckles white.

If he didn't know better, he'd think Blue had come up with this plan to torture his big brother. They should have decided to flip Nancy around, put her feet in his lap, instead of her head.

Well, it was too late now. There she was, and there *he* was, hanging on by a thread. Desire was raging through him like a prairie fire out of control, gaining heated power with every passing second.

He wanted this woman.

He wanted Nancy with an intensity far beyond anything he'd known.

That desire had been there from the moment he'd seen her, and had been steadily building, brewing, like a simmering cauldron threatening to boil over.

Oh, man, this drive into town was going to take an eternity, and he wouldn't bet a buck that he was going to survive it.

Tux glanced in the rearview mirror for the umpteenth time, seeing no sign of a vehicle behind them.

Should he tell Nancy that Butch wasn't following them, so she could get her head out of his lap? No, that wasn't smart. There were too many side roads on this stretch, and they could pick up a tail at any moment.

Relax, Bishop, he ordered himself. Think assignment. Think detached, clinical, just-doing-my-job-ma'am. Think about *anything* except the fact that he wanted, needed, ached to make love with Nancy.

Tux blinked, then watched his right hand, of its own volition it seemed, float off the steering wheel.

He redirected his attention to the road before he drove into a tree, as his fingers drifted down to sift through the dark, wild tumble of Nancy's hair.

Oh, yeah, his mind hummed, he could easily imagine how exquisite it would be to feel those silky strands dancing across his bare chest, followed by Nancy's soft lips; kissing, tantalizing, driving him closer and closer to the edge, then over it into ecstasy.

"Oh, Lord," he moaned, as he felt his manhood stir.

"Hmm?" Nancy murmured, a dreamy quality to her voice.

Tux smacked his hand back onto the steering wheel and ordered himself to leave it there.

Oh, too bad, Nancy thought. Tux had stopped playing with her hair. It had felt so good, was strangely soothing and erotic at the same time.

She'd made no further attempt to quell the heated desire swirling within her, had decided to savor it, not fight against it.

The entire scenario that had brought Tux Bishop into her life temporarily was bizarre, had an otherworldly quality to it.

And the key word in that conclusion was *temporarily*.

Tux was there only until the mystery of the blue shawl had been solved, then he'd be gone. She knew that. She accepted that. It was, in fact, the way it should be, as she wanted no part of a man being a *permanent* fixture in her existence.

She knew what she wanted for her life—*including* the wish to make slow, sweet love with this magnificent man.

So, Nancy? she asked herself. Why not? She was a mature woman with a modicum of sophistication. She was free, able to make her own choices and willing to take full responsibility for them. Tux was a consenting adult, who knew his own mind. Everything was in its proper place.

"We made it," Tux said, stopping the truck. He turned off the ignition and removed the key. "You're home, Ms. Pretzel.'' He paused and looked down at her. ''Nancy, did you fall asleep?''

She moved slowly upward, fluffing her hair with her fingers, and managing to scoot next to Tux in the process. She turned her head to look directly into his eyes, visible in the glow of the light over the back door of Buttons and Beads.

Nancy dropped her hands from her hair and wrapped her arms around Tux's neck.

''No, I'm not asleep.'' She leaned forward to speak close to his lips. ''I'm awake, Tux, very awake.'' She flicked her tongue over his lips. ''Are you...awake?''

Tux stared at her with wide eyes. ''What's wrong with you? Weren't you getting enough oxygen down there on the seat?''

''For Pete's sake.'' She yanked her arms free of his neck and folded them across her breasts. ''You're as romantic as a rock, Tux Bishop. Now I feel like an idiot, thank you very much.'' She bent over. ''Where's my button jar?''

In the next instant Nancy gasped in surprise as she was spun around by strong hands gripping her shoulders.

''Romantic? You want romantic?'' Tux said. ''Sitting in a junky truck by a bare lightbulb doesn't cut it, but it's the best I've got at the moment.''

''I...''

''Shut up.''

''Okay.''

''Good.''

And then Tux captured Nancy's lips in a searing kiss.

Nine

When Tux finally ended the kiss, his heart was pounding and his breathing labored. Nancy drew a much needed breath. Without speaking, they gathered their belongings and left the truck.

Encased in a sensuous mist, they entered the store and hurried up the stairs to Nancy's living room. The button jar, the blue shawl, Nancy's purse and Tux's Stetson, were placed on the sofa, then they moved eagerly into each other's arms, their lips meeting instantly.

Yes! Tux's mind hammered.

He lifted his head to take a sharp breath, then his mouth melted over Nancy's once again, savoring her sweet taste.

Yes, Nancy thought dreamily. Yes, yes, yes.

She parted her lips to receive Tux's tongue, meeting it with her own, stroking, dueling, heightening her passion to a fever pitch.

She'd waited so long for this night with Tux, for what it

was yet to bring. It had been an eternity since he'd walked into her store and her life, and awakened her slumbering femininity like never before.

It was right and it was good, because she was *choosing* to take this step. It was her decision, dictated by no one but herself, the responsibility of it hers alone.

Tux. He was there for now, would be leaving as soon as the mystery of the danger connected to the blue shawl was solved. She knew that, and she accepted it.

This night was theirs, separate and apart from the tomorrows to come.

Yes.

Tux broke the kiss. "Nancy?"

"Yes," she whispered.

"Are you sure?" he asked, his voice gritty. "I want you so damn much, but I have to know you're certain this is right for you."

"Yes, it is. I'll have no regrets, Tux, I promise. I want you very much."

He brushed his lips over hers, then they moved into the bedroom, where Nancy flipped back the blankets on the bed. The curtains were open, allowing the luminescence of the Texas moon to cascade over them with a silvery glow.

They removed their clothes quickly with hands not quite steady, then gazes swept over the other, bringing feelings of awe, wonder and anticipation.

Incredibly Beautiful Nancy, Tux thought. She was exquisite, perfect. Her breasts were full, her hips gently sloped, her legs long and slender. She was all, everything and more, that he knew she would be.

"You're beautiful," he said, looking directly into her eyes.

"So are you, Tux."

And he was. So tall, strong, proportioned so magnificently, it was as though he'd been chiseled from stone. Such wide shoulders he had, then ropy muscles in his arms and powerful legs. The curls on his broad chest were moist, and his surging manhood boldly announced his want of her.

Tux lifted Nancy into his arms, placed her in the center of the bed, then followed her down. He braced himself on one forearm, weaving his fingers through her hair with his free hand.

"I love your gypsy hair," he said.

Nancy smiled. "I'm not a gypsy."

"Oh, I think you might be. You're a spell weaver, Nancy. You've cast a spell over me. I have *never* wanted anyone as much as I do you."

"Then you're a spell weaver, too, because I want you more than I could ever begin to put into words. I'm on fire."

"Hot," he whispered. "Burning."

"Yes."

"Oh, yes," he said, then his lips met hers in a searing kiss.

As he deepened the kiss, Tux took his hand from Nancy's hair to cradle one of her breasts, gently stroking the nipple to a taut bud with his thumb. Moments later he ended the kiss to replace his thumb with his mouth, drawing the lush flesh of her breast within.

Nancy moaned softly in pure feminine pleasure, as her hands roamed over Tux's shoulders, the bunching muscles of his back, then upward again to sink into the thick, silky depths of his hair, urging his mouth harder against her breast.

She savored the exquisite sensations rushing through her, felt the pulsing heat deep and low within her that matched the seductive rhythm of Tux's tongue on the nipple of her breast.

Tux moved to her other breast and Nancy shifted restlessly as her passion soared, her hands now fluttering over him, touching, caressing like the delicate wings of a butterfly.

The blood pounded in Tux's veins. His racing heartbeat echoed in his ears. As he paid homage to the sweet bounty of Nancy's breast, his hand slid down her side, along the slope of her hip, then over to seek and find her moist heat.

"Tux," Nancy gasped.

He lifted his head to meet her gaze, his eyes nearly gray instead of blue, delivering in a smoky hue the message of his desire.

A groan rumbled in his chest as he saw Nancy's slightly parted lips, the flush on her cheeks, the enticing tumble of her hair on the pillow.

"You want me. You're ready for me," he rasped, hardly recognizing the sound of his own voice.

"Yes," she whispered. "Please. Oh, Tux, please."

He moved over her, wishing to postpone the moment, anticipate it longer, knowing he couldn't, as he slipped closer and closer to the edge of his control.

He kissed her once again, then entered her, watching her face, rejoicing in the soft, womanly smile that formed on her lips as her lashes drifted down.

"Oh, yes," she murmured.

Tux filled her and she received him, all of him, into the dark haven of her body. He stilled, struggling for command of himself, determined that Nancy's pleasure would come first, before he sought his own release. His muscles trembled from forced restraint.

Somewhere in the passion-laden mist in Nancy's mind, she realized what Tux was doing.

Sudden and unexpected tears stung her eyes. She felt so special, so cherished. Tux was thinking of *her* before himself, wanted to pleasure *her*, meet her needs before his own. He was giving her so much and she wished to return his gift in kind.

She gripped his sweat-slicked shoulders and lifted her hips.

"Nancy, no," he said. "Wait. I can't..."

"Together, Tux. We'll dance, we'll soar...together."

Tux's control snapped and he was lost. He began to move within her, the tempo increasing with every thrust, pounding, wild, thundering.

Glorious.

Nancy matched his rhythm beat for beat, felt the tension building within her in a spiraling coil, tightening.

On and on they went, higher and higher.

Searching.

Then finding.

"Tux!"

"Yes!"

A beat apart they reached the summit and were flung into oblivion, clinging to the other, holding fast.

They hovered there, wishing to stay forever, never to return. Slowly, so slowly, they drifted down, sated, spent, awed.

Tux collapsed against Nancy, then mustered his last ounce of energy to roll off her before he crushed her, keeping her close to his side.

Heartbeats quieted as bodies cooled.

Tux sifted his fingers through Nancy's hair, his lips resting lightly on her forehead. She splayed one hand on his moist chest, feeling his heart beating steadily beneath her palm.

"Incredibly Beautiful Nancy," Tux said quietly.

"What we shared was beautiful. I've never felt so... It was wonderful."

"Yes."

They fell silent, simply savoring. Then Nancy drifted off to sleep.

Tux frowned as the voice of reality began to buzz in his mind, demanding attention, refusing to be ignored.

The blue shawl. Danger. Butch looking for him for some unknown reason.

Tux eased carefully away from Nancy so as not to waken her, then pulled the sheet over them. He slid one arm beneath his head and scowled at the ceiling, which was visible in the silvery light still streaming in the window from the Texas moon.

He had never, he knew, experienced lovemaking as fulfilling, both physically and emotionally, as he had on this night with Nancy.

Why? Why had it been so different with her, so...complete? What did that mean? Why didn't he know?

Blue's words suddenly echoed in his head, causing his frown to deepen even more.

Nancy really is incredibly beautiful, just like you said she was. I sure do think she'd make a wonderful wife. You should at least discover what you two might have going together.

Blue just didn't understand, Tux thought. Blue had said he wouldn't care if UPS delivered someone like Nancy to him, as long as she arrived on his doorstep.

Well, not Tux Bishop. He hadn't asked for unbidden visions of a blue shawl, danger and Nancy. He hadn't *chosen* to have Nancy in his life. To him that was important, despite how nuts Blue considered him to be.

So, yeah, okay, the lovemaking he'd shared with Nancy had been beyond belief. And, yes, he cared about her, cared *for* her. But he had no intention of viewing her as a potential wife.

Besides, Nancy had a twisted view of what being in a relationship meant. She wouldn't want to be seriously involved with him, anyway.

He'd decided he was going to work on her attitude, make her see she had her facts wrong. It would give him something to do while he was protecting her, instead of just counting beads until he turned into a blithering idiot.

Did he still want to attempt to straighten out her thinking on love being a controlling force, taking something away from a person? Did he want to do that so Nancy would be receptive to the next man who entered her life?

Hell, he hated that thought.

Nancy was his.

Blue's grinning face flashed before Tux's mental vision.

Tux mumbled several earthy expletives, then shifted his gaze to Nancy, watching her sleep.

He wasn't going to think anymore tonight. His mind was a
heap of scrambled eggs. He was just going to look at Nancy
and remember the lovemaking they'd shared. Tomorrow was
soon enough to sift through the maze in his brain.

For now? There was only Nancy.

Moments later, Tux was peacefully asleep.

In the muted tones of predawn rose that cast a nearly ethereal aura over the room, they awakened, as though each had
been touched by a gentle hand urging them to emerge from
slumber.

They reached for each other with a naturalness usually born
of a multitude of mornings shared by lovers.

The urgency and raging need of the night had been quelled,
leaving glowing embers of desire that could be fanned at leisure into hot, burning flames.

And so their dance was slow, tantalizing, discoveries were
made and reveled in; taste, touch, aromas savored like one
would a rich, rare brandy.

When they joined at last, meshed their bodies into one entity, the rhythm was gentle and had a reverence that expressed
the unspoken wonder and awe of what they were sharing.

As they slipped over the edge together into glorious ecstasy,
they held fast to the other, knowing they shouldn't go to that
exquisite place alone.

They returned with matching sighs of contentment; sated,
complete, separate yet still one. They lay close, hands resting
on the other, connected, linked, and only then realizing that
not one word had been spoken, because none had been needed.

Tux laced his fingers beneath his head on the pillow,
vaguely aware of the sound of the shower running in the minuscule bathroom.

He would move, he thought, rather hazily, in four or five

years. Lord, he felt good. Both his body and mind were replete to the point of perfection.

Soul mates ... Destiny ... Nancy ... Destiny ... Nancy ... Soul mates ...

Tux shot bolt upright on the bed, the sheet slipping low on his hips.

Where in the hell had *that* come from? he fumed. He'd had that all squared away, had dealt with it, dismissed it. Nancy was *not* his soul mate, nor his destiny. A psychic fluke would *not* dictate the future of Tux Bishop.

"Damn it," he said, then threw his pillow across the room.

Nancy stood in the shower, vigorously shampooing her hair as she hummed softly.

Singing before coffee? she thought suddenly. My, my, wasn't it amazing what magnificent lovemaking could do for a person's personality?

She sobered as she rinsed her hair.

This was morning after inventory time. Was she sorry she'd made love with Tux? Did she have any of the regrets she'd promised him she wouldn't indulge in?

No.

After turning off the water, she stepped onto the bath mat and began to dry with a fluffy towel.

No, she mentally repeated, no regrets. What she'd shared with Tux had been beautiful beyond description. The memories were tucked away for safekeeping, hers to have for as long as she chose to cherish them. So be it.

She wrapped the towel around her like a sarong and returned to the bedroom, her hair wet and tangled. Tux was wearing his jeans and holding clean clothes against his chest.

"You can have the bathroom," she said, smiling. "I even left you some hot water."

"All right," he said gruffly, not looking at her.

Nancy frowned. "Tux? What's wrong? I'm the one who's

supposed to be grumpy in the morning before I've had my coffee, not you. Talk to me.''

He met her troubled gaze, no readable expression on his face.

''Talk to you about what?'' he said. ''It's morning, I need a shower and some breakfast. It's no big deal. Okay?''

A cold fist tightened in Nancy's stomach and a shiver coursed through her.

''Just…just what does your 'it's no big deal' encompass, Tux?'' she demanded, her voice quivering slightly. ''Everything?'' She swept one arm in the air in the direction of the bed. ''Everything?''

No! his mind hammered. Nancy looked so stricken, hurt, and the color had drained from her beautiful face. But he didn't know what to say, what to do. He was shaken to the core, so damn confused about his feelings for her.

Soul mates… Destiny…

He couldn't handle this! He was fighting a foe he didn't understand or know. He would *not* be dictated to by outside forces, but yet…

''Look,'' he said, ''what we shared was really great, but let's not get nuts here. You don't want any part of a serious relationship. You've made that very clear more than once.''

Nancy just stared at him.

''I'm here until the mess with the blue shawl is taken care of. That's it.'' He shrugged. ''So, we know where we stand. Everything is…fine, just fine.''

Nancy lifted her chin and ignored the ache of threatening tears in her throat.

''I see,'' she said. ''Yes, of course. You're right, Tux. We're mature adults who have chosen to have a brief, sexual affair. No strings attached. When it's over, it's over. Yes, everything is…fine.''

He nodded briskly, started across the room, then stopped.

''You'll have to open Buttons and Beads late today,'' he

said. "I have some things to check out, and I don't want you alone in the store with the front door unlocked. I'll get back here as soon as I can."

Nancy narrowed her eyes. "Wait just a minute, mister. No one tells me when I may, or may not, open my place of business. I went along with your ridiculous orders that caused me to become a pretzel in a pickup truck, but you're overstepping now. Buttons and Beads will open on time, just as it has for two years."

A muscle ticked in Tux's tightly clenched jaw. "Don't push me, Nancy."

"Push *you? You're* the one who's attempting to take control of my life."

Tux looked at the rumpled bed, then back at Nancy.

"I'm controlling your life?" he repeated. "That's not how I remember it."

"I didn't mean... I wasn't referring to..."

"Keep it separate, Nancy. Our lovemaking has nothing to do with the reality of the danger you're in. We're equal partners in that bed. In the blue shawl area, I'm in charge. Get that straight right now, because I'm not in the mood to fight you on the issue every inch of the way."

"Damn it, Tux, I—"

"The store stays closed until I get back," he said, then strode from the room.

"The hell it does, buster," Nancy said to no one.

Then she picked up the remaining pillow on the bed and threw it across the room.

Ten

While Nancy was in the kitchen sipping from a mug of much needed coffee, she heard Tux leave the apartment, closing the door none too quietly behind him.

"Fine," she said aloud, with an indignant sniff. "Act like a three-year-old throwing a tantrum, Tux Bishop. See if I care." She finished her coffee and thudded the mug onto the counter. "Oh, what an infuriating man."

Muttering under her breath and calling Tux several very unladylike names, she marched down the stairs and across the front area of the store with every intention of opening Buttons and Beads on schedule.

She smacked her hand onto the lock on the door, then stared at her fingers where they gripped the small metal bar, willing them to turn it from the hinge. But they wouldn't budge.

Sighing, she pulled her hand away, then pressed the fingertips of both hands to her temples.

She, she thought miserably, was the one acting like a spoiled brat.

Oh, darn, the whole thing would be easier to handle if she didn't believe in psychic powers. She could then accuse Tux of being on a macho power trip by telling her what she could and couldn't do.

But she *did* believe in psychic phenomena. The blue shawl was real, and so was the hovering, shadowy threat of danger.

Tux Bishop had literally put his own life on hold to protect her, stay close, see the bizarre situation through to its proper end. He didn't *have* to do all that, but he was.

She realized from what Tux, then later Blue, had said, that Tux's powers were an embarrassment to him, something he'd prefer to totally ignore. He was having to deal constantly with the reality of his unwelcomed gift.

She also knew that he hadn't left her alone that morning so he could go play nine holes of golf, or whatever. He'd been disturbed by the fact that Butch was looking for him, and was determined to find out why.

Ordering her to keep the store closed was due to the simple fact that Tux couldn't be in two places at the same time.

Nancy threw up her hands in defeat, walked away from the locked door, and went into the back room. Sitting down at the table, she slid the next order on the stack into place in front of her, then stared into space.

As long as she was being brutally honest with herself, she thought, she might as well admit the truth. She'd been hurt, crushed by Tux's declaration that their lovemaking was a temporary situation that would soon end.

She'd had no reason to react as she had, because what Tux had said was true; she did *not* want any part of a serious relationship.

Tux hadn't caused the ache of threatening tears in her throat, the cold fist of pain in her stomach. No, they had come from her own inner contradictions and confusion.

When it came to Tux Bishop she was a muddled mess.

Every time she thought she once again had her head on straight about Tux it turned out not to be the case.

That wasn't Tux's fault, it was hers.

"Oh, what am I going to do with me?" she said aloud, shaking her head. "For now? Count beads. It's two, four, six time, Nancy Shatner."

She looked at the first item on the order sheet.

"Five dozen beads, Color G-2," she read aloud.

G-2, she mentally repeated. That was the code for a certain shade of green.

This was Friday, green day, representing luck. How appropriate. She would definitely be thinking green while waiting for Tux to return.

Tux sat in his office at Bishop Investigations. He laced his fingers behind his head, leaned back in the leather chair and stared at the ceiling.

Why, he asked himself for the umpteenth time, was Butch trying to locate him? How long would it be before he got tired of waiting for Tux to leave Blue's ranch? It was understandable that the hood preferred not to possibly take on the entire crew of the Rocking B, but how much time would the visible sports car buy? And who was Butch working for these days?

Tux jerked forward and folded his arms on the top of the desk, glowering at the wall across the large room.

This was going to take some digging, he thought, and possibly a great deal of time on the streets. While he was gathering information about Butch, he was *not* protecting Nancy.

Nancy had done one of two things: kept the store locked as he'd ordered her to do, or mentally told him to take a flying leap and opened Buttons and Beads as per her usual routine. Either way, he needed to get back to the store pronto.

Tux dragged both hands down his face and sighed.

Lord, he'd acted like a jerk before he'd left Nancy's. He'd

been so damn shook up about his confusing feelings toward her, and he'd taken it out on her.

He'd bellowed orders at her like a drill sergeant, knowing full well that Nancy had a thing about being told what to do.

What he *should* have done was sit her down, quietly explained why he had to leave for a while, then *requested* that she keep Buttons and Beads closed until his return. For all he knew, she believed he'd gone to play a round of golf, for Pete's sake.

And if that wasn't bad enough, he'd acted like a bed-hopping sleaze, as he'd informed her that the sex was great, but don't get ideas about a good old-fashioned romp in the hay.

Tux shook his head in self-disgust.

He owed Nancy an apology. No, he owed her several apologies. How did a man go about making peace with a feisty, strong-willed woman like Nancy? He didn't have the foggiest idea.

He punched a button on the intercom on the corner of his desk.

"Frank?" he said.

"Yes."

"How's your day shaping up?"

"Not bad. I'm finishing a couple reports, then I'm doing a stakeout tonight. Need something?"

"Yeah, I do. I need some help. I can't be in two places at once."

"Figured that out, huh, Tux? Reality stinks, doesn't it? What's cooking?"

"Find out everything you can about a hood for hire named Butch," Tux said. "Who is he working for now? What's the word on the street about why he's looking for me? See if the name Nancy Shatner rings any chimes in connection with Butch."

"Got it."

"Call me on my beeper when you have something. Thanks, Frank."

And between now and when he arrived back at Buttons and Beads, Tux thought, he had some *very* serious thinking to do about Nancy.

After receiving telephone calls from Glenna and two other merchants on the block expressing concern as to why Buttons and Beads wasn't open, Nancy had taped a sign to the front door. It read: Busy, Busy. If You Need Me, Knock.

Left in peace, she'd proceeded to practice apologies to Tux, while dutifully counting beads.

So far, she'd rejected every "I'm sorry" speech she'd come up with, thoroughly depressing herself.

Just before noon, a sharp knock sounded at the back door of the store. Nancy jumped in surprise at the sudden noise, causing the frosting spatula to skitter through a pile of beads, sending them flying in all directions.

"Tux," she whispered, staring at the door. "Oh, dear, this is it."

She got to her feet, straightened her red-and-white sports top over her jeans, and marched to the door, ignoring the trembling of her knees.

"Yes?" she said, when she reached the door.

"It's Tux."

She unlocked the door and pushed it outward so Tux could enter. As he stepped inside, the door swung closed behind him, and Nancy's eyes widened in shock.

Tux was carrying a large flat box that was causing the delicious aroma of hot pizza to waft through the air. On top of the box was a brown sack, and clutched in one of his hands was a long-stem red rose circled with green florist paper.

"Hi," he said, not smiling.

Nancy's eyes swept over the cargo he carried, then she met his gaze.

"Hi," she said, not smiling, either.

"Nancy, look, I..." he began.

"Tux, I want..." she said, at the same time.

"Go ahead," he prompted. "You first."

"Oh. Well, I..." She took a deep breath. "I'm sorry about this morning. I threw a tantrum, I was very unfair, I left the store locked like you told me to, and I hope you'll accept my apology." She gulped in some much needed air. "There."

Tux frowned. "*You're* apologizing to *me?* I came bearing gifts to apologize to *you.* I acted like a jerk before I left here, and I'm really sorry."

"Oh," she said, appearing confused.

"Could I set this stuff down?"

"Yes, yes, of course."

She hurried to the table to sweep the scattered beads onto the mat. Tux set the box on the table, then took a six-pack of soda from the sack. He extended the rose toward Nancy.

"Peace?" he said, smiling.

Nancy matched his smile and accepted the rose. She brushed the velvety soft petals over one cheek, then inhaled the delicate aroma.

"It's beautiful," she said, looking at Tux again. "Thank you. I'm going to run upstairs and get something to put it in before it wilts."

Tux nodded. "I'll spread out this gourmet lunch. Grab some napkins while you're up there. Please. If you want to, that is. Only if you feel like it."

Nancy laughed. "Okay."

A short time later they were murmuring in pleasure as they took the first bites of the pizza. The rose stood majestically on the table in a water-filled peanut butter jar.

"Delicious," Nancy said. "Do you know how long it has been since I've had greasy, gooey pizza? It has been centuries."

Tux chuckled. "That long, huh?"

"Yep."

"Nancy, do you want me to unlock the front door?"

"No, not yet. I want to enjoy every bit of this. People on the block were calling to see if I was all right. I finally put a sign on the door. Another twenty minutes won't matter."

"I like the way all of you look out for each other. It's nice."

Nancy smiled. "In this neighborhood, it's definitely comforting. I must say, though, that we've been very fortunate about never having had any trouble. There *are* street gangs in this area. My Pollyanna brain likes to think that the gang members actually respect the fact that we've cleaned up our storefronts and are trying to make something of ourselves."

She shrugged.

"I'm probably dreaming. The gangs no doubt know we don't have enough money at any given time to make it worth their while to rob us."

"You never know," Tux said. "Street gangs have codes they operate by. Your Pollyanna thinking might be right on the mark. I don't suggest you track down any of the gang members and ask them, though."

"Oh, okay."

They ate in silence for several more minutes, then Tux drained his soda can and thunked it onto the table.

"Nancy," he said quietly, "we need to talk."

She wiped her fingers on a napkin, then met his gaze. "What do we need to talk about?"

"Everything. We've apologized to each other for what happened this morning, and I suppose we could put it all behind us, case closed. I don't like that, though, because it doesn't explain what set me off and caused me to act like a jerk."

"Is it important?"

Tux nodded. "Yes, I believe it's very important." He stared at the far wall for a long moment, gathering his thoughts, then looked at her again. "I was reacting to my reaction to you."

Nancy leaned slightly toward him. "Pardon me?"

"Oh, boy," he muttered, dragging a restless hand through his hair, "this is going to be tough."

He folded his arms on the top of the table and looked directly into her dark eyes.

"Nancy, when we made love, I was deeply moved emotionally. Physically it was sensational, beyond my scope of experience. But the emotions were foreign, strange and... Hell, I don't even know what half of them were, what they meant, what I was supposed to be understanding.

"I was shook up, really rattled, and I reacted by lashing out at you. You have become very special to me, very quickly, and I'm having a problem dealing with that."

"I see," she said softly, then paused. "No, I don't. Why don't you like the idea of my being special to you?"

He held up one finger.

"One. You don't want to be involved with anyone, be *special* to anyone."

Another finger popped up.

"Two. I didn't find you on my own. My male ego says *I* decide which woman is in my life. I'm not going to be dictated to by short-circuited psychic powers. However, that reasoning is starting to seem rather lame."

"It is?" Nancy said, her gaze riveted on Tux's face.

"Yeah, it is." He covered one of her hands with one of his on the top of the table. "I know you care for me, Nancy. You wouldn't have gone to bed with me unless you cared. It would have had to truly be making love, because you don't do casual sex."

"No. I mean, yes." She shook her head. "No, I don't engage in casual sex and, yes, I do care for you, about you. But..."

Tux sighed. "But you don't want to be in a relationship with me, or any man, because you view it as having to give away a part of yourself. You see it as handing over the control of your life to a man, being accountable for everything you do and say.''

"Yes."

"No. That's not how it is. It's not, Nancy. You're comparing a relationship with a man to the struggle for independence you have going with your mother. That's apples and oranges.''

"No, it isn't.'' She pulled her hand from beneath his. "A person is either free, or they're not. If I agree to be in a committed relationship with a man, be half of that couple, then half of me is no longer mine."

"You're forgetting about what *he's* giving to *you*. It blends together, give-and-take. Now you have more because of what you're receiving."

"That doesn't make sense. Besides, what makes you such an expert?"

Tux raised both hands. "This isn't a call to arms. We're having a mature discussion."

"Sorry," she muttered.

"I'm *not* an expert, because I've never been in love. However, I've had the privilege of observing my parents for over three decades. I've seen how it works when it's done right.''

Tux smiled gently while Nancy waited for him to gather his thoughts.

"My folks are unique individuals,'' he finally said. "What it takes for each to be fulfilled within themselves is so different that it's day and night. Yet when they're together, they're each *more* than they were alone. More than whole. The frosting on the cake. The cherry on the whipped cream. The jimmies on the chocolate sauce."

"That's how *you* perceive it. I believe that one of them sacrificed, lost something, to be in that marriage all these years."

Tux shook his head. "No. Ask Blue or Bram about our parents if you don't believe me." He paused. "No, better yet, meet my folks for yourself. We'll go over there tonight. Okay?

My mom would get a real kick out of looking at those buttons in your junky jar.''

"It's a very lovely jar," Nancy said absently, then frowned. "Tux, why are you doing this? Why the hard sell on serious relationships being the greatest thing since sliced bread?''

"Because every five or ten years, Blue says something intelligent, and I guess he was due. He told me it shouldn't matter *how* you came to be in my life, the important thing is that you're here. He also said that I should get off my ridiculous macho trip, and make an attempt to at least discover what we might have together. That's a tad tough to do if you insist on being an apple, while I'm an orange.''

"But…''

Nancy stopped speaking as Tux got to his feet and came around the table. He gripped her upper arms gently and drew her up close to him, wrapping his arms around her. She splayed her hands lightly on his chest and looked at him questioningly.

"The other reason I'm sounding like a nagging old woman,'' Tux continued, "is because your attitude is so far out in left field it's a crime. It really needs a major adjustment. I'm asking you to think about the fact that you just might be wrong.''

"Or I just might be right,'' she argued, frowning slightly, "and you should change from an orange to an apple.''

"What you definitely are is stubborn, Ms. Shatner." He brushed his lips over hers. "Nancy, say you'll think about what I said. That's not too much to ask, is it?''

"Think about the possibility that a serious relationship might add to my life, instead of taking a part of me from being…well, mine?''

"You could even go a little further than that.'' He kissed her quickly, then trailed a ribbon of kisses across her cheek and down the side of her slender throat. "You could view that relationship as *us,* you and me. You could be discovering what we might have together at the same time I am.''

A shiver coursed through her as Tux repeated the tantalizing foray with his lips on her other cheek, then down her throat. The rippling shiver turned instantly into heat, causing a warm flush to stain her cheeks.

''Will you do that, Nancy?'' Tux said, close to her lips. His voice was low and rumbly, and very, *very* male. ''Will you set aside your etched-in-stone attitude for a while, and view all this with an open mind? There's no great risks to run by *thinking,* is there?''

He outlined her lips with the tip of his tongue. Nancy trembled in his arms.

''Is it possible that a relationship *is* the frosting on your cake? Is it possible that a relationship could be you and me, together? I, for one, have decided I've had enough of this confusion. I want some concrete answers as to what is happening between us. I decided that between buying the rose and getting the pizza.''

He kissed her deeply, passionately.

''I...I can't think at all when you do that,'' she whispered, hearing the thread of breathlessness in her voice.

''Just say yes. Say you'll agree to take a fresh look at your attitude *and* you'll consider, discover, what we might have.''

''But...''

Tux slid his hands over the slope of her buttocks, nestling her to the cradle of his hips.

''Yes?'' he prompted.

''Oh...yes,'' she said, desire sweeping throughout her.

''Good. That's good. Discovery, Nancy. That's what we're embarking upon here. Right?''

''Right,'' she said dreamily.

Tux claimed her mouth again in a searing kiss. Nancy melted against him, entwining her arms around his neck, returning the kiss in total abandon.

For the first time since Buttons and Beads had been born, the store stayed closed for an entire workday.

It was Friday, green day, for luck.

Eleven

When Nancy and Tux finally emerged from her apartment, they ate dinner at a pleasant family restaurant. While they were waiting for their food to be served, Tux telephoned his mother to ask if it would be convenient to bring Nancy over to the house. He added that they'd be bringing a jar of buttons, too.

Jana-John was delighted at the prospect of meeting Nancy, and also said she'd adore seeing the buttons.

Before long, Jana-John, Abe, Nancy and Tux were finishing off big bowls of ice cream. The foursome had chatted comfortably during dessert, and Nancy had decided instantly that she liked Tux's parents very much.

Tux carried the ice-cream bowls and spoons to the kitchen, then returned to pop open the tightly stuck lid on the jar.

"Oh, dear," Nancy said, peering in the bottle, "there's so much dust and lint in here. If I dump out the buttons it's going to make an awful mess."

"Understandable," Abe said. "Back in history, the family

button jar was tucked into the ever-present mending basket. It stands to reason that it would be kept open for easy access, therefore collecting dust and what have you.''

"We've finished reading today's newspaper," Jana-John said. "I'll spread it out on the table and solve the problem."

Jana-John completed the task, then Nancy tipped the jar over slowly, making a trail of buttons down the center of the table.

"Goodness," Nancy said, setting the empty jar next to her. "I never dreamed there were so many buttons in that jar."

Jana-John began to flatten out the few buttons that had fallen on top of others.

"Don't you wish these buttons could talk?" Jana-John said. "Just think of the stories they could tell."

"Hey, look at this," Tux said, picking up a button. "It's a bottle cap with the rough edges hammered down. Someone poked a couple of holes in it and used it as a button. I'll be damned, that's really something."

"Here's a pretty one," Nancy said. "It has a tiny piece of tatting glued onto it."

"Oh, let me see," Jana-John said. "That is exquisite. Abe, isn't this lovely?"

"It certainly is, my dear," Abe said, smiling. "As is seeing how lovely you look when your eyes are dancing and your cheeks are a soft pink. *You* are exquisite, my darling wife."

"Thank you, my love," Jana-John said, reaching over to give his hand a quick squeeze.

Tux nudged Nancy's foot under the table, causing her to look at him. He leaned back in his chair with a very smug expression on his face.

"Jimmies on the chocolate sauce," he said. "Right?"

"Yes, well…" Nancy conceded, "I guess you're right, but it's rare, very rare, the exception to the rule."

"Not necessarily," he said. "I believe there's a lot of frosting on cakes and cherries on whipped cream out there."

"Tux, dear," Jana-John said, appearing rather confused. "Are you hinting that you'd like more ice cream? You know you don't have to ask. Just go get it."

Tux laughed. "No, Mother, thank you. I've had plenty. Enjoy the buttons."

For the next half an hour, Nancy, Jana-John and Abe examined the buttons, all three having a marvelous time.

Tux was content to watch Nancy, savoring the sight of her childlike excitement, the ease with which she interacted with his parents, the rightness of having her next to him in the home where he grew up.

Incredibly Beautiful Nancy, he mused. Was she really meant to be his, his future, his forever, his wife? Was Nancy his destiny?

He didn't know, but he'd moved past fighting with himself over how she'd come to be in his life. Now he was centering on what they might have together, the discoveries he'd make.

"Oh," Nancy said suddenly, "I recognize this woman."

"What?" Tux said, pulled from his musing.

Nancy pointed to the newspaper in front of her.

"That woman was in the ladies' room at the restaurant where we ate, Tux. She got into the car being driven by that Butch person. You remember her, don't you?"

Tux leaned toward Nancy to look at the picture in the newspaper.

"Not really," he said. "I was having meaningful eye contact with Butch. What does it say there under the picture?"

Nancy moved her hand to read the caption.

"It says, 'Reputed criminal, Jimmy Denton, leaves the courthouse with his attorney. Accompanying the pair is Denton's secretary, Candace Malone. Denton was cleared of charges of fraud.'"

"Figures," Tux said, straightening again in his chair. "They can never convict slick Jimmy Denton." He chuckled.

"Secretary? I doubt that Candy darlin' has ever typed a word in her life. She's Denton's mistress."

"I see," Nancy said thoughtfully. "Now it makes sense. Candace was furious because a man she called Jimmy the Jerk had stood her up. He had an important meeting with someone from New York. Candy was really... Achoo! Excuse me. The dust from the buttons is tickling my nose."

She reached down next to her chair, lifted her purse onto her lap, then began to rummage through the large tote for a tissue.

"Do you keep food for a week in that purse?" Tux said, smiling.

"Now, Tux," Jana-John explained, "there are things a woman needs to have with her at all times. Men simply don't understand that."

"True," Nancy said. "I..." She stopped speaking and removed her hand from the purse. "This ring isn't mine. I've never seen it before."

Tux extended his hand palm up. "Could I see that?" Nancy dropped the large ring into his hand. "Whoa," he said, examining the piece of jewelry. "This is the real goods. Take a look at this, Dad."

Abe accepted the ring, studied it, then nodded. "Indeed it is. The diamond is surrounded with emeralds, rubies, sapphires, and it's all set into very fine gold. It's a bit gaudy in my opinion, but I'd estimate its worth to be approximately a hundred thousand dollars, give or take a few thousand."

"What?" Nancy said, nearly shrieking.

"Nancy," Tux asked, "do you have any idea where this ring came from?"

Nancy's hands flew to her cheeks and her eyes widened.

"Yes," she said, "yes, I do. Oh, mercy, Candace Malone must have put it in my tote when we were picking up our belongings after our purses fell to the floor.

"Candace was upset because of being ignored by Jimmy

Denton *and* because he'd said she couldn't wear the ring in public. Oh, my gosh, she said I'd just won the lottery.''

"Holy smokes," Tux said, then got to his feet. He began to pace restlessly around the table, a deep frown on his face. "It works. Yes, it fits together."

"Tux?" Nancy said.

He continued his trek.

"Tux!"

He jerked at Nancy's outburst, stopped, and looked at her.

"What?" he asked. "Were you talking to me?"

"I need *you* to talk to *me*," she said. "This is bizarre."

Jana-John smiled at her. "Angry people often do bizarre things, dear. I'm sure Candace regrets her impulsive actions by now."

"And Butch has been sent to retrieve the ring," Tux said. "He's not looking for *me*, Nancy, he's trying to find *you*. I'm his link to where you are, because he saw us together. *This* is the danger I sensed in my visions."

"Oh, dear heaven," Nancy said, feeling the color drain from her face.

"Don't panic, Nancy," Tux said. "I…" A series of dinging noises interrupted Tux. He looked down at the beeper attached to his belt, memorizing the number inching across the tiny screen. "I need to use the phone."

As Tux left the room, Nancy drew a trembling breath.

"Everything is under control, my dear," Abe said, patting her gently on the shoulder.

"Oh, my, yes," Jana-John added, smiling brightly. "You don't have a thing to worry about, Nancy. You just sit back, relax, and leave everything to my darling boy."

"I can't do that," Nancy said, a near-frantic edge to her voice. "I really *am* in danger. I have the blue shawl, now there's this awful ring and… *I* have to take steps to protect myself."

"That doesn't make sense," Jana-John said, obviously confused. "You're with Tux now. When two people are together, each should do what they do best. Tux is an expert at dealing with men like Butch, at protecting those who aren't trained to handle potential danger."

"It's like the diapers," Abe said.

"I beg your pardon?" Nancy said.

"Well," Abe went on, "when the boys were babies, I was a whiz at feeding them, giving baths, playing games, you name it. But diapers? No matter how hard I tried to pin those cloth menaces on, they fell off the minute I picked up whichever son was the current victim of my clumsy fingers. I could *not* put on a diaper."

"Exactly," Jana-John said. "Each person does what they do best, give-and-take, sharing. I tended to all the diapers, but Abe was a tremendous help in the other areas of raising three busy little ones. Do you understand now, Nancy? Let go of your feminine pride. Allow Tux to take care of you until this danger is dealt with."

Before Nancy could reply, Tux returned to the table.

"That was Frank from my outfit. There is absolutely nothing being said on the street about Denton, Butch, the ring…nothing at all."

"Which means what?" Nancy asked.

"That Denton is keeping it under wraps to save face," Tux said. "It's a tad embarrassing to have your mistress pitch a fit and give away a ring you gave her as a gift. A ring worth a lot of money. Denton will want this settled very quickly, very quietly. Interesting."

"That's not the word I would have used," Nancy said miserably. "Try terrifying."

"We have the upper hand, Nancy," Tux explained. "Denton wants this kept hush-hush, and we have the opportunity to shout it from the rooftops, give the story to the press, or whatever."

"What we're giving," Nancy said, getting to her feet, "is

the ring back. Let's go find Butch or Candace, and hand it over. Right now.''

Tux shook his head. ''No. I'm not running any risks by not knowing the mood Butch is in, or the orders he might be following that Denton gave him. I figure, though, that Butch is out of time and patience. He's going to go to the Rocking B, because my car is still there. Blue has his script. He'll follow the directions I gave him, will hesitate, then finally tell Butch that we're at the store.''

Jana-John looked pointedly at Nancy. ''Blue will follow Tux's orders, Nancy, because Tux is the expert at the moment. Tux, however, wouldn't tell Blue how to ride a horse.''

''What?'' Tux said.

''Never mind, dear,'' Jana-John said. ''Nancy knows what I'm talking about.''

''What's the next step in your plan, son?'' Abe said to Tux.

''I'm going to call Blue and bring him up-to-date. He'll let me know the minute Butch has been at The Rocking B.''

Tux paused.

''Legally,'' he continued, ''the ring is yours, Nancy. Candy gave it to you of her own free will. You have every right to keep it.''

Nancy clutched her hands tightly in her lap and stared down at them.

''I'll settle for being alive,'' she whispered.

''Hey,'' Tux said.

He closed the distanced between them and hunkered down next to her chair, covering her hands with his.

''Nancy,'' he said, ''all this came to a head very quickly, and it's a lot to digest. Just take it slow and easy. But do know this. Nothing, *absolutely nothing,* is going to happen to you, because I'll be with you every second. Understand?''

Nancy hesitated a moment, then nodded.

''Diapers, diapers, diapers,'' Abe muttered. ''Never did get the hang of them, but it really didn't matter because Jana-John was an expert at diapers.''

Tux pushed himself to his feet and frowned at his father.

"Are you feeling all right, Dad?" he asked. "We're really not discussing baby diapers here.''

"Yes, we are," Jana-John said merrily. "Go call Blue, darling. Does anyone want some more ice cream?''

Tux chuckled, shrugged in confusion at what his mother was talking about, then his smile faded.

"Nancy and I will have to pass on more ice cream,'' he said. "I want to call Blue, then get back to Nancy's place. I'll need a little box for the ring, if you have one. Nancy, would you please put the buttons back in the jar?''

Tux headed for the telephone. Jana-John and Abe went in search of a small box for the ring.

Nancy sighed, propped one elbow on the table, planted her chin in her hand, and began to drop the buttons into the jar.

"Two, four, six," she counted. "This is the story of my life.''

Her life, she thought, as she continued to tend to the buttons, was once again completely out of her control. For a tick of time after she and Tux had apologized for their rotten behavior, she'd felt as though she were a partner, fifty-fifty, in the scenario they were involved in.

Not only that, but during the lazy and glorious afternoon of exquisite lovemaking with Tux she'd believed herself to be the woman to his man, equal, half of their whole.

But now? Dear heaven, she was on brain-circuit overload again. She was supposed to sit quietly in the corner like a good little girl, while to protect her, Tux squared off against a thug?

While attempting to comprehend Tux's theory of her changing from an apple to an orange, of understanding the frosting that was to ice her cake, she was now dealing with Jana-John and Abe's dissertation on why Abe had never changed diapers, and how that made the senior Bishops' relationship so much stronger.

"Oh, good Lord." Nancy sighed, smacking the lid on the now-filled jar. "This is too much, it really is. I've had it. I quit. I'm going to Siberia, or New Jersey, or..."

"Let's go," Tux said, reappearing at the table and interrupting Nancy's mumblings.

"Here's a nice little box," Jana-John announced, coming back into the room with Abe. "It even has cotton in it." She removed the lid, nestled the ring inside, then replaced the lid. "There." She looked up to see that both Nancy and Tux had one hand extended to receive the box.

"Thank you, Jana-John," Nancy said, lifting her chin.

"I'll take the box," Tux told his mother.

Nancy's head snapped around and she looked at Tux, her dark eyes flashing.

"No, you won't," she said, "because what you're taking is complete control of my life again. You're not discussing, you're dictating. You take some time off, then...wham... you're back in your I'm-in-charge-here mode."

When Tux didn't respond, Nancy rushed on.

"Well, I've had enough of your behavior, Tux Bishop. I have so much to deal with right now, and the last thing I need is for you to do a machismo trip at this point."

Nancy folded her arms over her breasts and glowered at Tux.

"Did you, Mr. Bishop, ask me if I wanted you to take possession of *my* ring? No. Do I understand why we're returning to Buttons and Beads to be sitting ducks for that gruesome man, instead of you and your trained investigators going to him? No. Do I think your apples-should-be-oranges, and cakes-can-have-frosting theories are a bunch of baloney? Yes. Yes, yes, yes."

Jana-John and Abe swiveled their heads simultaneously toward Tux, as though they were watching a tennis match.

A flash of temper swept through Tux, and he opened his mouth, ready to deliver an angry retort to Nancy's tirade. In the next instant, he clamped his mouth shut again.

Easy does it, he told himself. If he didn't cool it, he and Nancy would be smack-dab in the middle of a rerun of this morning's debacle.

The thing was, Nancy was right. Yes, he now knew what they were facing, and it would be a helluva lot easier if Nancy would just step back and allow him to take charge of the situation.

But she was *not* about to do that. So…okay…he'd respect that. And he'd respect her need to be included and informed.

Nancy Shatner, he thought, *here's a serving of jimmies on your chocolate sauce, coming right up.*

Tux smiled his hundred-watt number, his charming-to-the-max smile.

"You're absolutely correct, Nancy," he said. "I was out of line. The ring is technically yours. Where would you like to put it for safekeeping for now?"

Nancy blinked in surprise. "Oh. Well, I guess it would be safer with you than me."

"Fine," Tux said, still beaming. "I'd prefer to return to Buttons and Beads. You see, if we're on our turf, that gives us the advantage of being one step ahead. The bad guys don't know that the good guys know what the bad guys know. You know what I mean?"

Nancy nodded slowly. "Yes, I think I do. Well, fine. We'll go to Buttons and Beads." She burst out laughing. "This is ridiculous. *I'm* ridiculous, but thank you, Tux. We're still doing everything your way, but I feel included in the decision-making process."

"Which is how it should be," he said, his smile completely gone. "I'll get the hang of this, Nancy. I'm trying, I really am. Be patient with me, okay?"

She smiled at him warmly. "Okay."

"Which only goes to show you," Abe said.

"Yes, dear?" Jana-John said.

"There's more than one way," Abe said, "to solve the dilemma of the diapers, my love."

By the time Nancy and Tux returned to Nancy's apartment, she was so exhausted she felt as though she couldn't take another step. She sank onto the sofa with a wobbly sigh.

Tux sat down next to her, slid one arm across her shoulders and shifted her gently to him, nestling her head on his chest.

Nancy sighed again and snuggled closer, not wanting to think about anything, just wishing to feel the comforting strength of Tux.

"Everything is going to be fine," Tux said quietly, sifting his fingers slowly through her hair. "I know this is frightening, Nancy, but it will all be over soon. Nothing is going to happen to you. You believe that, don't you?"

"I guess so."

"You *know* so." Tux paused. "Tomorrow is Saturday. Will you open the store?"

"Yes, I work on Saturday, then I'm closed Sunday and Monday. I usually fill some orders on those days, but I'm free to grocery shop, go to the Laundromat on the next block, clean the apartment, all kinds of fun stuff."

Tux chuckled, causing Nancy's head to bounce a bit on his chest.

"Sounds like a thrill a minute," he said.

"How long do you think it will be before Butch shows up here?"

"Not long. I realize the waiting will be hard on your nerves, but that's how the game is set up. Blue will let me know when Butch comes to the Rocking B, which will give us some advanced warning."

"I just want this nightmare to be over," Nancy said, "finished, done. Tux, give Butch the ring the minute he walks into the store.''

"No. I want to see how this plays out, what Butch's story is.''

Nancy lifted her head to look directly into Tux's blue eyes.

"Tux, please, give it to him. It's my ring, you said so yourself. I can decide what to do with it.''

Nancy moved farther back, straightened, then framed Tux's face in her hands. Tears filled her eyes and echoed in her voice when she spoke again.

"Oh, Tux, I couldn't bear it if something happened to you. The ring isn't worth putting your life at risk. Don't you understand what I'm saying, how I feel? I...''

Nancy stopped speaking and shook her head, as tears choked off her words.

Tux stared at her, his racing heart seeming to grow to nearly bursting within his chest.

What was he to understand? he wondered. What *was* Nancy saying to him? Did Nancy love him? Was she *in love* with him? Lord, what an incredible thought. It was... Yes, it was fantastic! There was a warmth suffusing him from head to toe. There was a chance, there really was, that Nancy had *discovered* that she loved him.

Destiny. Soul mates.

Whoa, Bishop, he ordered himself. Slow down. Before he went nuts here, he'd better tap into his own emotions, find out what *he'd* discovered about his feelings for Nancy.

Love? Had he fallen in love with her? Well, hell, how was a guy who'd never been in love supposed to know if he'd gone and done it, fallen in love?

He was willing to lay his life on the line for Nancy, in a way not remotely close to how he'd felt during an assignment as an agent. That had to mean something important.

He wanted to be with her, protect her, share, talk, make love, hear her laughter, see her smile. He'd rather be near her than away from her. He wanted to stay as close as possible to her whenever he could.

And with every breath in his body, *he wanted her to be deeply and irrevocably in love with him.*

Holy smokes, this was it, it had to be. *He was in love with Nancy. Destiny. Soul mates.* Yes!

Should he tell her how he felt, what he'd just *discovered*, then press her to declare her feelings, whatever they were, for him? No, not now, he decided.

She had too much to deal with right now. First he'd settle this business of the psychic visions, the blue shawl, the danger, and the damnable ring.

Then he and Nancy would have some serious talking to do about the future.

About forever.

He was going to ask Nancy Shatner to be his wife and the mother of his children. Nancy would be his, he would he hers, until death parted them. She *was* his destiny. She *was* his soul mate. He loved her!

"Tux?" Nancy said, bringing him from his jubilant thoughts. "I can tell that you're thinking very seriously. Will you do it? Give the ring to Butch when he comes?"

"What?" He shook his head slightly to clear it, and Nancy dropped her hands from his face. "No. Nancy, look, there are principles involved. I don't curl up and yell uncle at the first sign of trouble. The ring is legally yours. I refuse to just turn it over on demand to a hood who is throwing his weight around."

"But..."

He brushed his lips over hers. "Shh. Don't worry, or at least try not to. Nothing will happen to you, or to me, either for that matter. Trust me."

Nancy sighed.

Tux frowned, suddenly realizing it was extremely importan

to him that Nancy *did* trust him. Trust was a major part of a relationship—of a marriage.

"Do you?" he asked. "Trust me?"

Nancy hesitated a moment, then nodded slowly. "Yes. Yes, Tux, I trust you."

"Ah, Nancy, thank you," he said, then captured her lips with his.

For the first time in his life, Tux thought, he was kissing the woman he loved. He wanted to remember this kiss, he really did.

Then all rational thought fled as desire exploded within him, hot and churning, and he deepened the kiss.

Nancy encircled Tux's neck with her arms, returning the kiss in total abandon.

She felt, she thought hazily, like a teetering tower of children's blocks. One thing after another had been added to her tower, causing it to grow taller and more unsteady.

And now? She, herself, had placed yet another block on the wavering stack.

When she'd pleaded with Tux to give the ring to Butch, when she'd said she couldn't bear it if something happened to him, the words had come from the very essence of her heart and soul.

She'd been filled with immeasurable fear, an icy wave of terror born of the knowledge that harm might come to the man she...

Loved?

Nancy jerked, breaking the kiss. She stared at Tux with wide eyes.

"No," she said, not realizing she'd spoken aloud.

No! She was *not* in love with Tux Bishop, refused to be, wouldn't even consider the possibility. She could not, would not, turn over her life to Tux, be only half of who she was, no longer be in control of her total being.

"Nancy?" Desire radiated from Tux's eyes. Confusion was

evident on his face. "What's wrong? Don't you want to make love?"

"What? Oh, yes, yes, Tux, I want to make love with you," she said. But she did not want to be *in* love with him.

Nancy leaned forward to press her lips to Tux's, parting them to slip her tongue inside his mouth to seek and find his tongue. A groan rumbled in Tux's chest.

Moments later, Tux ended the kiss, lifted Nancy into his arms as he rose from the sofa, and carried her into the bedroom.

In a flurry of motion, the blankets on the bed were swept back, and clothes were shed.

Don't think, Nancy ordered herself. Forget the tower of teetering blocks. Forget everything. Except Tux. Just feel, just feel.

Think, Tux's mind hammered. Remember every detail of what was about to come. He was going to make love with the woman of his heart, his life's choice, his love. He wanted to have these memories for all time.

They tumbled onto the bed with matching, raging need, wanting...wanting...wanting. They kissed, caressed, tasted, hands and lips never still, always moving, savoring, *discovering*.

The heat within them burst into licking flames, consuming them with passion.

"Please," Nancy whispered, with a near sob.

Tux thrust into her, deep, giving her all that he was, receiving all that she gave.

The rhythm of their bodies as they moved as one was wild and pounding, synchronized to perfection. The tension within them coiled and thrummed, bringing them closer and closer to what they sought.

What they found...together.

They were flung over the edge, calling to each other, holding fast to each other, rejoicing in each other.

Then they drifted slowly back and without speaking, gave way to the somnolence that claimed them.

When Nancy awoke the next morning, she turned her head on the pillow to look at Tux. The expanse of bed next to her was empty. Her gaze fell on a piece of paper resting on Tux's pillow.

She snatched it up and read the message aloud to the empty room.

"N. Went down the block for groceries. Back in a flash. You sleep pretty. T." Nancy laughed. "Hear that, world? I sleep pretty."

In the next instant she sobered, a frown replacing her delighted smile.

Back to reality, she thought, throwing off the blankets and leaving the bed.

She went into the bathroom and was soon standing under the warm spray of water in the shower. After dressing, putting on her usual light makeup, and pouring a mug of coffee from the pot Tux had made, bless his heart, Nancy decided to telephone her mother to take care of the promised weekend call.

Sitting on the lumpy sofa, she dialed the familiar number.

"Hello?"

"Good morning, Mother," Nancy sang out. "How are you on this lovely Saturday? Did you know that in the world of beads, this is black-and-white day, representing organization?"

"Oh?" Ruth Shatner said. "Well, I'm glad you told me that, dear. I've been having a dickens of a time trying to decide what to wear. I have a very smart black-and-white suit that will do nicely."

"Are you doing something special today?"

"I'm going out to dinner this evening with... Well, it's only dinner, but a woman does like to look her best for any occasion. I'm having my hair done this afternoon. Goodness, it has been years since I've gone to the beauty parlor. Organization day? Well, fine, I feel very organized.''

"Out to dinner?" Nancy said. "Are you going with the ladies from your bridge club?''

"Well, no, dear. You remember Mr. Henderson from down the street? His wife passed away about five years ago. We bumped into each other in the grocery store and started chatting. The next thing I knew, Fred asked me out to dinner.''

Nancy jumped to her feet, nearly pulling the telephone off of the end table.

"You have a date with a guy named Fred? A real date?''

"There's no need to yell, Nancy.''

"Oh. Sorry.'' Nancy sank back onto the sofa. "I'm just surprised, that's all.'' She paused. "And pleased,'' she added quickly. "I'm just tickled pink.''

"I'm looking forward to it. I must dash, dear. I want to make a nice dessert. I thought I'd invite Fred in for coffee and dessert after we dine.''

Nancy's eyes widened. "You're going to invite him in for coffee on your first date? Now, Mother, listen to me. Things have changed tremendously since you were dating Dad. You'll be conveying a message by asking Fred in for coffee tonight.''

"Oh, posh, don't be such a stick-in-the-mud. I watch television, you know. I'm aware of what's happening out there in the singles scene. I must go, dear. I have so much to do. Have a lovely, organized day. Goodbye for now.''

"Bye.''

Nancy stared at the receiver, hearing the dial tone humming. She clunked the receiver into place, then took a big swallow of coffee.

Unreal, she thought incredulously. Her mother hadn't nagged about Nancy moving back home. In fact, Ruth Shatner hadn't really had time to talk to her because she was preparing for a date with Fred What's-his-name.

"That's wonderful,'' Nancy said aloud.

Was Ruth changing into an orange from an apple? Was she going to *discover* what she might have with good old Fred, and allow her daughter to live her own life as Nancy saw fit?

Unbelievable. But most definitely possible.

The telephone rang and Nancy jerked, nearly spilling her coffee. She picked up the receiver.

"Buttons and Beads," she said.

"Hey there, Incredibly Beautiful Nancy, this is Blue. Tux around?"

Nancy smiled. "Good morning, Blue. Tux should be back any second. He went down the block to get some groceries."

"No joke? If he works up to doing windows, let me know. My place could use some scrubbin' and rubbin'."

"Don't get so excited," she said, laughing. "My cupboards were sadly bare. Tux went to the store out of desperation. Shall I have him call you?"

"No, I'm heading out of here. Listen, tell Tux his buddy came looking for the owner of the spiffy sports car bright and early this morning."

Nancy stiffened and a cold knot tightened instantly in her stomach.

"Oh?" she managed to say.

"He was dripping charm," Blue went on. "His spiel was that he's considering buying a car like Tux's, and wanted to ask some questions about it. What a bunch of bull."

"What did you tell him?"

"I followed Tux's instructions to the letter. I was cautious at first, then did my 'aw, shucks' routine and gave Butch the name and address of your store. You and Tux are getting company today. Guaranteed."

"Oh, good Lord," Nancy said, pressing one hand to her forehead.

"Hey, sweetheart, calm down. Tux can handle this situation with no sweat. You just follow his orders, and this nightmare will be over before the Texas sun sets. It'll be a done deal, the final chapter written.''

"I'm fine, really I am. I'll tell Tux everything you said, Blue.''

"Okay. See ya, Nancy.''

"Goodbye, Blue,'' Nancy said, then replaced the receiver.

The final chapter? she thought. She already knew what it was, how all of this would end.

Tux Bishop would no longer be in her life.

Nancy Shatner would be totally and chillingly alone.

Twelve

Nancy had worked herself into a nervous-wreck frenzy by the time Tux returned to the apartment, carrying two large sacks of groceries.

Her mind was fragmented. A portion was chilled with fear that Butch was surely going to make an appearance at Buttons and Beads that very day.

Another section was dark and gloomy at the prospect of Tux leaving her life, because she had no choice but to send him away.

And a minuscule part was still whirling from the telephone conversation with her mother.

The minute that Tux stepped into the living room, Nancy began to chatter like a magpie, relating everything that Blue had said. Tux listened and nodded as he put the groceries away. He made himself some toast, then settled at the table with the plate of toast and a mug of coffee.

Nancy sat down opposite him, leaning forward and looking at him questioningly.

"Well?" she said.

"I make a great pot of coffee," Tux said. "I hope you've noticed that fact."

Nancy smacked the table with one hand, causing Tux to cringe.

"Tux Bishop," she said, none too quietly, "don't you dare pull an I'm-macho-and-cool routine on me. I want to know what we're going to do. That horrible man is coming here…probably with a gun…to get the ring. I bet he left Blue's ranch and headed straight for Buttons and Beads without stopping for breakfast or anything else."

"Yes," Tux agreed, then polished off a piece of toast.

"How can you eat at a time like this?"

"I need all my strength," he said, cocking one eyebrow at her, "to survive a session of your hollering your head off."

"Oh." Nancy sank back in her chair, then lifted her chin. "I'm sorry I hollered. I'm calm now." She cleared her throat. "Tux, I would appreciate your sharing your plan for dealing with the unsavory man who is due to arrive here at any moment."

Tux chuckled. "Certainly, ma'am. It's really very simple." He glanced at his watch. "You're supposed to open the store in ten minutes. I'd like to say that you're to stay up here while I go downstairs, but that would be a waste of words."

"Do tell," she said, frowning at him.

"I *am* telling you. We're going to compromise. You'll be in the back room down there. You'll remain in said back room until such time as I say you can leave it. There won't be a peep out of you, because Butch won't be aware of the fact that you're in the back room." He grinned at her. "Please."

"But…"

"Oh, and thank you in advance for your wise and mature cooperation in this matter. I know you wouldn't do anything other than what I'm asking you so politely to do, because I need total concentration while doing my part of the plan. Right? Right. We're all set, a team, the dynamic duo, ready to roll.''

"But…"

Tux got to his feet, leaned across the table to give Nancy a toe-curling kiss, then carried his dishes to the sink.

"Let's do it," he said. "Where's the blue shawl? I'd like you to drape the shawl around your shoulders, if you would be so kind. I know it's rather warm for a shawl, but your wearing it has two purposes."

Nancy crossed the room to stand in front of Tux.

"Which are?" she said, looking up at him.

"A psychic phenomenon is a mystery unto itself. So, one…by your wearing the shawl, Butch may hurry it up even more to get here, which is fine with me.

"Two. I saw you with the shawl in my original visions. I'm hoping the images will be gone for good if a detail like that is covered now."

Nancy nodded. "I understand."

"Good. Are you ready to go downstairs?"

Nancy placed both hands flat on Tux's chest and gazed directly into his blue eyes.

"Please be careful, Tux," she said softly. "Promise me you will."

He encircled her with his arms. "I promise." *I love you.* "Nothing will happen to me." *Because I plan to marry you and spend many, many years by your side.* "Don't worry." *Just love me.*

Tux lowered his head and captured Nancy's mouth, kissing her until their breathing was labored and hearts were racing. Tux finally broke the kiss, very reluctantly.

"Whew," he said. "Talk about blowing my concentration. You'll have to stop kissing me for now, but keep the thought handy for later."

"Mmm," she said dreamily.

"We're outta here," he announced, moving around her. "You're now two minutes late opening the store. Shame on you. You'll never make Businesswoman of the Year at this rate."

Nancy blinked, then hurried after him, coming to a halt in the living room. Tux was clipping a holstered gun to the back of his belt.

A cold fist tightened in Nancy's stomach.

Tux shrugged into a lightweight, dark blue windbreaker to conceal the weapon.

A shiver coursed through Nancy.

"Nancy, get the shawl," Tux said. "Okay?"

She nodded, unable to speak as the ache of unshed tears closed her throat.

Oh, Tux, her mind whispered. *Oh, my Tux, please, please be careful. You're so much more important than that ring, no matter how much money it's worth. You're more important than anything in this world, and I love you with all my heart.*

"What?" Nancy said, her eyes widening.

Tux frowned. "Hey, are you with me? The blue shawl?"

"Oh, yes, yes, of course," she said, hurrying to collect it.

Don't think, she told herself. She was in love with Tux? *Oh, good Lord, don't think. Not now.*

With shaking hands, Nancy clutched the shawl as she followed Tux from the room.

As Tux placed one foot, then the next, on the stairs leading from Nancy's apartment to the store below, he began to shift mental and physical gears.

His senses went on red alert, his muscles were tensed and ready for action, his mind was focused on confronting Butch, who would arrive to demand the return of the ring.

By the time he and Nancy entered Buttons and Beads, Tux

was in his agent mode, prepared to kill rather than be killed, if it was necessary.

"Go into the back room," Tux said to Nancy. "Remember—stay out of sight no matter what happens."

Nancy stared at Tux for a long moment.

"Tux?" she said tentatively. "Are you all right? You seem, I don't know, *different* somehow."

"I'm fine," he said, his eyes flickering toward the front door. "Go. I want to open the store."

Nancy hurried to the rear area and sank gratefully onto a chair at the table, her trembling legs refusing to support her for another second. She draped the blue shawl around her shoulders.

Two, four, six, she thought giddily. Not a chance. There was no way on earth she would be able to do anything more than sit there quaking in terror until this nightmare was over.

Tux crossed the room to unlock the front door. As he flipped the sign to Open and unsnapped the lock, he muttered an earthy expletive.

Holy smokes, he thought, look at that. The big man himself was coming to collect that damnable ring.

A black limousine with dark tinted windows had just parked in front of Buttons and Beads. Butch and another huge man got out, then Butch opened the rear door of the expensive vehicle. A woman and a man emerged to stand on the sidewalk.

"Jimmy Denton," Tux said quietly, "has come to call, with darlin' Candy in tow."

Nancy got up carefully from the table and crept to the side of the doorway, flattening herself against the wall, wanting to hear every word that was spoken in the front of the store. She gripped the blue shawl between her breasts with both hands.

*   *   *

Jimmy Denton was short, about five feet seven or eight inches tall, wore a custom-tailored caramel-colored suit, a dark brown shirt, and a caramel tie with brown stripes.

Around fifty, his thinning hair was a dull salt-and-pepper. His nose was too big for his face, his eyes too small, his mouth a thin, cruel slash.

Candace stood head and shoulders above Denton, and wore a blue silk dress that accentuated her voluptuous figure.

One of the men stayed by the vehicle, while Jimmy, Candy and Butch started toward the door of Buttons and Beads.

Tux moved quickly to stand behind the row of bins of beads.

Jimmy Denton, he thought, might look like a wimp, but he had a reputation for being a powerful, dangerous and ruthless man.

Gear up, Bishop. The fact that Denton himself had come for the ring said that the sleaze wanted it very badly and would stop at nothing to get it.

Damn, Tux thought, he should have left Nancy upstairs. He should have demanded, ordered, begged, whatever it took, to get her to remain safely behind the locked door of the apartment.

Nancy, he mentally directed, *stay put in that back room. Don't make a sound, not a peep. Oh, Lord, Nancy, please.*

The door to Buttons and Beads opened, the bell tinkled its cheerful greeting, and the parade entered: Butch, Jimmy Denton and Candace. The trio stopped in the center of the room, Denton sandwiched between the other two.

"Good morning, Mr. Bishop," Jimmy said, his voice smooth and silky. He smiled for a second, but the false gesture didn't reach his eyes.

Tux nodded slightly. "Denton."

"You don't seemed surprised that I know who you are," Jimmy said. "I also know *what* you are."

Tux shrugged. "Anyone can run plate numbers. Did you have a productive meeting with your New York buddy the other night?"

Denton frowned, then quickly composed himself, flashing his phony smile again.

"Well done, Tux," Jimmy said. "I could use a man like you on my payroll."

"No, thanks," Tux replied. "Want to buy some beads?"

"Let's not play games, shall we?" Jimmy said. "I've come for the ring. *You* know that, *I* know that. Hand it over, and I'll be on my way."

Tux crossed his arms loosely across his chest.

"Well, Jimmy," he said, "I'm afraid I can't do that. In the first place, the ring belonged to Candace. Secondly, she chose to give it to someone else. End of story."

"Candy acted irrationally," Jimmy said, "as women are known to do. She was impulsive, and created a situation that needs to be rectified. *Now.* Hand over the ring."

"No," Tux said.

"I am *not* an irrational female," Candy shouted at Jimmy. "You gave that ring to me, and I had the right to do whatever I pleased with it."

"My point exactly," Tux remarked. "You drove all the way down here for nothing, Denton. See you. Oh, goodbye, Candy, Butch."

"Bishop," Denton said, "I'm a busy man. I want the ring...now."

"Can't do it, Jimmy," Tux said. He dropped his arms to brush back the windbreaker and plant his hands on his hips. "The ring has a new owner, who will decide whether to wear it, or sell it."

Jimmy glanced at Butch, who immediately produced a gun that was pointed at Tux. In the next instant, Tux shifted and his own weapon was revealed.

"Butch can shoot me, Denton," Tux said, a steely edge to

his voice, "but this gun is squared off right at your heart. Before I go down, you'll be a dead man. I'll also be dead, I suppose, but since I'm the only one who knows where the ring is, killing me wouldn't be very smart."

"Ah, but your lady, your lover, who owns this trashy place," Jimmy said, "must be aware of the location of the ring. I don't need you, Bishop."

Trashy place? Nancy fumed. *Trashy place!* The nerve of that man. How dare he say such a thing about her business, her Buttons and Beads. And how dare he threaten to shoot her Tux.

She'd...had...enough!

In a blur of blue-shawl motion, Nancy ran out of the back room.

"Aaak!" she screamed at the top of her lungs.

Everyone jerked in surprise.

"You people are ridiculous," Nancy raged. "Look at you, for Pete's sake, with your tough-guy guns and... You've all been watching too much television." She paused. "Hi, Candy. I'm Nancy."

"It's nice to see you again," Candy said pleasantly. "Are you enjoying the ring?"

Nancy sighed. "Not really. It's the cause of an awfully messy situation here. Would you like to have the ring back?"

"No," Tux said.

"Yes," Jimmy said.

"This is between Nancy and me, James," Candy snapped, glaring at Jimmy. "You treated me very badly the other night, and I'm seriously considering ending our relationship once and for all."

Jimmy paled. "Now, honey bun, don't say such a thing. I love you, adore you, worship the ground you walk on. I promise I'll never break a date with you again."

"And the ring?" Candace prompted.

"Hell, do whatever you want with it," Jimmy said. "It's just a trinket. You can have a dozen others if you want."

"Fine," Candy said stiffly. "I'm glad we understand each other."

"Do you understand *me*, Denton?" Tux asked. "If we cross swords in the future, don't push."

"Yes, yes," Jimmy said, an impatient edge to his voice. "You've made your point. Butch, put the gun away."

Butch did as instructed, then Tux slowly replaced his own gun in the holster.

"So, Candace?" Tux said. "Your call. Whatever your decision is about the ring is the way it will be."

"Well," she said, tapping one long, red fingernail against her chin. "The ring brings back memories of a very upsetting night in my life. I don't want the thing."

"Oh, Lord," Denton muttered.

"Nancy," Candace said, "I'll trade you the ring for that gorgeous shawl you're wearing. It'll go perfectly with this dress."

"But…" Nancy said.

"Sold," Tux said.

"No!" Jimmy yelled.

"James," Candace said, a warning tone to her voice.

Jimmy threw up his hands in defeat. "All right, all right. Do whatever you want."

Candy sashayed across the room, and a wide-eyed Nancy slipped off the shawl and handed it to her.

"Lovely," Candace said. "I'm happy now, Jimmy. Shall we go?"

"Wait just a darn minute," Nancy said. "I want an apology from that man for calling Buttons and Beads trashy. Threatening to shoot the man I love wasn't very nice, either."

Jimmy Denton rolled his eyes heavenward. "Women. Bishop, yours is as hard to deal with as mine. Nancy, as for my planning to kill the love of your life, he was going to shoot me, too. We're even on that one. But I do humbly apologize for making such a derogatory remark about your charming little store."

"I accept your apology," Nancy said.

"Goodbye," Jimmy snapped.

Jimmy, Candy and Butch left the store. Moments later the limousine sped away.

Nancy turned to Tux. "Hi," she said, smiling brightly.

Before Tux could reply, Nancy Shatner did what any brave, courageous and bold, red-blooded woman would do under the circumstances...she fainted.

"Oh, Lord." Tux's reflexes kicked in and he scooped Nancy into his arms as she began to crumple. "Nancy?" he said, holding her tightly to his chest. "Nancy? Please, sweetheart, speak to me."

Nancy's lashes fluttered, then she slowly opened her eyes, drawing a shuddering breath at the same time.

"Tux?" she whispered.

Before Tux could reply, bedlam broke loose.

The front door of the store crashed opened and the baker from down the block entered carrying a rolling pin. Glenna was right behind him, both hands wrapped around a baseball bat. The grocer had a shotgun, and the owner of the pawnshop was dragging a heavy sledgehammer.

Tux's sports car appeared out of nowhere, the tires squealing as it came to a halt, producing Blue and Bram.

"We saw the gangster car with the dark windows," Glenna said breathlessly. "It took a while to gather our weapons. Oh, darling Nancy, are you dead?"

"No, I'm not dead," Nancy said, propping her head on Tux's chest. "Hi, Glenna."

"So?" Blue said. "We came to the rescue. Anyone need to be rescued?"

"Nope," Tux announced. "Everything was settled very peacefully."

"You told Denton the facts of life, huh?" Bram said. "I knew he didn't need our help, Blue, but you wouldn't listen."

"Actually," Tux amended, "Nancy and Candace, Denton's lady, negotiated the deal. One blue shawl was traded for one *very* valuable ring." He shrugged. "Go figure."

"That's what Candy wanted to do," Nancy said. "It doesn't make much sense, but it's certainly better than having everyone shooting each other."

Man, oh, man, Tux thought, a grin breaking across his face. He looked at Nancy where she was nestled against him, safe in his arms. He loved this woman more with every passing second, tick of the clock, beat of his heart. She was really something, his Incredibly Beautiful Nancy.

And *she* loved *him.*

He'd heard her say it.

She'd told Jimmy Denton that his threatening to kill the man she loved was not a nice thing to do.

Hot damn, Nancy was in love with him.

Unreal. Unbelievable.

Fantastic!

Nancy smiled at him, and Tux thought his heart was going to jump right out of his chest.

"You can put me down now," she said.

"Do I have to?" he asked, matching her smile.

"I think you'd better."

"You didn't follow my orders, Ms. Shatner. What happened to staying out of sight and being quiet as a mouse?"

"I forgot. That man was really getting on my nerves."

"You are one dynamite lady." Tux kissed her quickly, then set her on her feet.

"Well, we're outta here," Bram said. "I've got a building to build."

"Thank you," Nancy said. "All of you. You're wonderful."

"Hey, Blue," Tux called, "leave my car here and take that heap of junk you said was a truck."

"Yeah, yeah," Blue said. "Give me the keys. Come on, troops, let's clear the deck."

A short time later, Tux carried two mugs of coffee to the table in Nancy's kitchen. He set one in front of her, then settled onto the chair opposite her. The small box containing the ring was near the edge of the table. Buttons and Beads was closed, Nancy having decided she'd earned the day off.

Tux took a sip of coffee, then looked at Nancy.

"The nightmare is over," he said. "You didn't follow the program in the visions, though. The blue shawl matched up, plus the rows of beads, but you were supposed to be scared to death."

"I was," Nancy admitted. "But then I got mad and sort of lost it. Oh, well."

Tux stared into his mug for a long moment, then met her gaze again.

"Nancy," he said seriously, no hint of a smile on his face. "Nancy, I love you. I want to marry you, spend the rest of my life with you, have a bunch of babies with you. I'm asking you to be my wife." He paused. "Nancy Shatner, will you marry me? Please?"

The color drained from Nancy's face as she stared at Tux.

"Just say yes," he went on. "We'll work out all the details later, like what you want to do with the ring, where you might like to relocate Buttons and Beads, what kind of house we'll buy, stuff like that. But first, please, say you'll marry me. I know you love me. You even told Jimmy Denton that you do."

"What?" she said, leaning slightly toward him. "I told Jimmy Denton what?"

"Don't you remember telling Denton he was threatening to kill the man you love?"

"No, I don't remember saying that. A lot of what happened downstairs is a blur."

"That's very understandable. But you *do* love me, don't you?"

"Yes. Yes, I do, but..."

"Then it's settled. You'll marry me?"

Nancy got to her feet, shaking her head. "No. No, I can't. I can't." Tears filled her eyes. "I didn't mean to fall in love with you. I don't want to be in love with you, Tux."

Tux got up and reached toward her.

Nancy raised both hands.

"No, please, don't touch me," she said, two tears spilling onto her cheeks. "I can't think straight when you touch me. Oh, Tux, don't you see? Nothing has changed."

"Yes, it has, damn it. We're in love with each other!"

"That doesn't matter! We don't have a future together, because I can't give a part of myself away. I won't lose a portion of who I am. I need all of me, Tux, to survive." A sob caught in her throat. "You have to go, Tux. Please. You have to."

The expression of shock on Tux's face shifted to a flash of anger, then pain, raw pain, settled over his features and in the depths of his blue eyes.

Without saying another word, he spun around and strode from the room. Moments later the sound of the apartment door slamming echoed through the empty rooms.

"Goodbye, Tux," Nancy whispered. "Goodbye, my love."

Then she sank onto the chair, lowered her head onto folded arms on top of the table, and wept.

Thirteen

Tux slouched in the chair behind the desk in his office and frowned at nothing, except his frame of mind.

Two weeks, he thought. It had been two long, lousy weeks since that awful, final scene in Nancy's apartment. Every painful detail of it was still so bitingly sharp, it might as well have taken place today.

Tux sighed.

He'd never see Nancy again. It hurt. Lord, how the truth of that fact hurt.

"You're dead meat, Bishop."

Tux's head snapped up at the sound of the threatening voice, and he saw Blue and Bram enter his office. Bram had delivered the less than cordial greeting. The twins settled in the chairs opposite Tux's desk and propped their ankles on their knees. They glowered at their older brother.

Tux matched their expressions. "To what do I owe the dubious honor of this visit? I just saw you ugly guys at Mom and Dad's for dinner last night. Don't you have work to do, or something?''

"Damn straight we do," Bram said, "but you know the drill. You can screw up your life all you want to until you step over the line.''

"Which you did," Blue said. "You have upset our mother.''

"Oh, hell," Tux groaned. He leaned back in his chair and stared at the ceiling.

"Rules are rules," Bram said. "If Jana-John Bishop is worried about one of her baby boys, the other baby boys have license to step in. *No one* stresses out our mother. That's the way it has always been.''

Tux looked at his brothers again. "Yeah, I know, I know. I thought I was doing a better job last night of covering up.''

"Oh, right," Blue said. "Your entire contribution to the dinner conversation was, 'Yep,' 'Nope,' 'Pass the salt,' and 'Nancy who?'. Mom caught me and Bram before we got out the door after you left. She's upset about whatever it was that happened between you and Nancy.''

"I don't need this," Tux said, dragging one hand through his hair, "but if one of you had upset our mother, I'd be all over you, too.''

"Yes," the twins said in unison.

"I just need some time," Tux said. "Okay?"

"No," Blue said. "Are you in love with Nancy?"

Tux sighed. "Yes. Oh, yes, I'm in love with her. I even asked her to marry me.''

"And?" Bram prompted. "Doesn't Nancy love *you?*"

"She loves me," Tux said quietly, fiddling with a pencil. "Yes, Nancy is in love with me.''

"Color me stupid here," Blue said, "but what's the problem then?" He shrugged. "You love her, she loves you, and they lived happily ever after. Right?"

"Wrong." Tux broke the pencil in half. "Nancy sees marriage as turning the control of her life over to someone else. She wants to be free, she says. Being in love, married, whatever, would deny her that freedom.''

"Is that nuts?" Blue said, to no one in particular. "Yes, I do believe that is nuts.''

"Whew," Bram said. "Your Nancy has an attitude.''

"Tell me about it," Tux affirmed. "She thinks like an apple. I think like an orange.''

"Huh?" Blue said.

"Opposites, dope," Bram said to Blue.

"Freedom?" Tux said. "Try this on for size. Nancy has no doubt made arrangements to sell the ring, and will soon be a very wealthy woman. Money can buy a helluva lot of freedom.''

Blue and Bram nodded.

"Look," Tux said, "I'm sorry I upset our mother, but you can tell her that I'll be all right in time. There's no hope for me and Nancy. None.''

"I'm sorry, Tux," Bram sympathized.

"Yeah, me, too," Blue said. "I really liked Nancy. I wish it would have turned out differently, Tux.''

"Yeah, well…" Tux said.

The twins got to their feet.

"Take all the time you need to get over this," Bram instructed. "We'll reassure Mom that you're not going to go off the deep end, or whatever.''

"Time, time, time," Blue said. "It's supposed to heal all wounds, you know. Bram's right. Take all the time you need.''

The brothers said their farewells, then Tux stared at the empty doorway that Bram and Blue had gone through.

"Take all the time I need?" Tux whispered to no one. "What if it's the rest of my life?''

Late that night, Nancy threw back the blankets on the bed and got to her feet with a groan of frustration.

Another tossing and turning, endless stream of hours, she fumed, stomping across the room to the window. Ah, yes, here she was again, staring down at the littered alley, the garbage and graffiti center of Houston.

"Oh, Nancy," she said wearily, "would you please get a grip?"

She missed Tux so much. She loved Tux so much. And she was such a muddled mess, it was ridiculous.

Wrapping her hands around her elbows in a protective gesture, she shook her head in self-disgust.

She needed protecting from *herself,* not an outside force. Her confusion was draining, both physically and emotionally exhausting.

She couldn't face another day spent chasing her own thoughts around in her mind in an endless circle. Tonight, darn it, she was going to reach some concrete conclusions as to what on earth was the matter with her.

She drew a steadying breath, squared her shoulders, and lifted her chin. Then, as though pulled by an invisible magnet, her eyes shifted from the ugly alley to look up, up, at the silvery Texas moon glowing in the black velvet sky that was sparkling with diamondlike stars.

"Texas moon," she whispered. "Tux's moon."

Tux. Tall, strong but gentle, magnificent Tux.

He had made her laugh right out loud and produce smiles that were genuine. He caused a warm feeling to consume her by doing nothing more than walking into the room.

They'd shared lovemaking so beautiful it defied description in its splendor.

Tux had enfolded her into his family, made her feel as though she were a part of the Bishop clan and, therefore, the recipient of their open and honest caring.

He had brought so many riches into her life that were to be cherished, treasured, as the precious gifts they were.

He had given her...

A soft gasp escaped from Nancy's lips as she continued to stare at the moon.

What Tux had added to her existence was like jimmies on the chocolate sauce and frosting on the cake.

Tux hasn't robbed her of her freedom, her independence, her voice. She was a woman in love, who was still an entity unto herself.

By loving and being loved in return, she was even more than she had been before Tux had walked through the door of Buttons and Beads. She'd grown, learned how to give of herself.

Oh, yes, she was free, very independent, standing alone as she'd decreed she must in order to be happy and fulfilled. Her cake was baked, whole, constructed as she saw fit by her own force of will.

But her cake had no frosting.

Her life had no Tux.

And she was lonely.

She wanted to have what Tux gave to her, give what Tux received from her. She wanted to be with the man of her heart for all time, be his wife, his equal partner, the mother of his children.

Tears filled Nancy's eyes at the same moment a gentle, peaceful smile formed on her lips.

"Thank you," she said, to the silvery Texas moon.

She turned and walked slowly back to the bed, pulling the blankets over her.

Was it too late? she thought. Would he forgive her for sending him away, for causing him the pain she'd seen in his expressive blue eyes? Had her fears and doubts caused her to lose the only man she had ever, would ever, love?

Nancy drifted off into a restless slumber.

The next afternoon, Tux's secretary whizzed into his office and plunked a small box in front of him on the desk.

"Package for you," she announced. "It was delivered by messenger."

Tux glowered at the square, white box. "So, what is it?"

"My X-ray vision isn't up to par today, boss," she said. "I suggest you open it if you want to know what's in it. Brilliant deduction, huh? I amaze myself sometimes with my own level of intelligence. Bye." She spun around and left the room.

"Nobody likes a smart mouth," Tux called after her.

"Sure they do," she hollered back, from beyond his view. "Open the box, for Pete's sake."

"Whatever." Tux smacked the pen he was holding onto the desk, and removed the lid to the box to reveal green tissue paper. "In the bead arena, green is for luck. Yeah, right. Fat chance."

He brushed aside the paper, then his heart skipped a beat before beginning to race wildly. Without even realizing he'd moved, he rose to his feet, then lifted out the contents of the box with both hands, as though he was cradling something made from delicate china.

It was a key chain. The quarter-size circle was comprised of tiny beads, each a different color, each having its own meaning. The creation had been laminated so expertly, it appeared as though the beads were floating in space.

"Oh, man," he said, his voice unsteady. "Nancy?"

"Yes, Tux...Nancy."

Tux looked up quickly to see Nancy walking slowly into the room. She closed the door, then stopped halfway across the large expanse. She was wearing an ankle-length, navy blue flared skirt and a pale blue blouse.

"Nancy, what..."

Tux suddenly realized he was standing there like an idiot with the gift in his hands.

He put the key chain back in the box, then came around his desk, sliding one hip onto the edge and folding his arms loosely over his chest.

Easy, Bishop, he told himself. *Don't go nuts.* He wanted to rush to where Nancy stood, scoop her up, and kiss her senseless. He'd missed her so damn much. He *loved* her so damn much.

But Nancy had smashed his heart to smithereens, caused him emotional pain like nothing he'd even known existed. She was here for a purpose...obviously, and he was keeping his big mouth shut until he found out exactly what it was.

"Tux," Nancy said quietly, "I'd like to talk to you. Please."

He nodded, no readable expression on his face.

Dear heaven, Nancy thought, Tux looked so closed, so unapproachable, as though there was a thick, solid wall surrounding him. Her legs were trembling so badly she had no choice but to go sit in one of the chairs in front of his desk, which would give him the advantage of looming over her. Oh, dear.

She moved to a chair and sank onto it gratefully, drawing a steadying breath in the process.

Nancy, she mentally ordered, *get a grip.* What she said in the next few minutes would very likely determine her entire future.

"Tux, I love you," she said, looking directly at him. "Do you believe that? Do you believe that I love you?"

Tux nodded again, meeting her gaze, but giving no clue as to what he was thinking.

"I know that I hurt you very badly," Nancy went on. "*You* became the victim of *my* doubts, *my* fears. I was so certain that if I followed my heart and allowed it to lead me into a serious relationship, a marriage with you, I'd lose part of myself."

"I know all this, Nancy," Tux said, a rough edge to his voice. "It has been beating against my brain for over two weeks. I can live without hearing it again."

"Yes, of course. I'm sorry." She stared down at her tightly clasped hands for a moment to gather her courage, then met his unreadable gaze again. "I've been so confused, so muddled. I haven't been sleeping well, and have spent hours at night looking out the window at the alley behind Buttons and Beads.

"But then last night I felt a tug, a pull of some sort, telling me to look upward, to look at the gorgeous, silvery Texas moon, *your* moon. It was while gazing at the moon that everything fell into place for me. I finally comprehended what you had been trying so hard to make me understand."

Tux's heart was beating so rapidly he could hear the echo of it in his ears. He forced himself to stay exactly where he was and maintain his blank expression.

"And?" he said, striving for a semibored tone of voice.

"I'm a complete woman. I'm me. Loving you, being your wife, won't take anything away from who I am." Unwanted tears filled Nancy's eyes. "I know that now, Tux, I truly do. You'd be the frosting on my cake."

Two tears slid down Nancy's pale cheeks, and she dashed them away.

"Tux, I'm asking you to forgive me for the pain I caused you." A sob caught in her throat. "I love you with all my heart. I want to be your wife, the mother of your children."

Tux moved so fast he nearly fell over his own feet. He gripped Nancy's upper arms, hauled her to him, and kissed her. His kiss was rough, urgent, born of the heartache and loneliness of the past two weeks.

But then the kiss gentled and Nancy returned it in kind, this kiss speaking of pain forgotten, joy, and hope for a future…together. Desire burst within them with hot, licking flames.

Tux encircled Nancy with his arms; she entwined his neck with her hands. The kiss deepened even more.

Tux finally broke the kiss, his breathing ragged. He framed Nancy's face in his hands and looked into her dark eyes.

"You're positive?" he said, his voice gritty with passion.

"Yes," she said breathlessly.

"And Buttons and Beads?" Tux asked.

"I'd like to move it to a safer neighborhood."

"Guaranteed. Will you marry me?"

"Yes. Yes, yes, yes."

"What about the ring, Nancy? All the money it will bring you? The freedom and independence that money could buy?"

"We'll sell the ring and decide together what to do with the money."

Tux grinned. "That's great. I love you, Nancy Shatner, with all that I am, I swear I do." He paused. "Want to have a baby?"

She matched his smile. "Sure."

"Good. That's good. When will you marry me?"

"Tuesday."

"What?"

"I'll marry you on Tuesday," she said, "and I'll wear a pink dress."

"Is Tuesday pink day in the bead world?"

"Yes."

"What does it stand for?"

"Oh, my darling Tux, Tuesday is pink day for true love."

He smiled at her warmly, making no attempt to hide the tears glistening in his blue eyes.

"My Incredibly Beautiful Nancy," he whispered, "we're going to have a lifetime of Tuesdays."

"Under the Texas moon," she said, smiling, as tears of happiness filled her eyes.

And then they sealed their commitment to forever with a searing kiss.

Epilogue

"**O**h, my stars, here I am snifflin' and needin' my hankie, due to my bein' so happy for Nancy and Tux.

"They truly did get married on a Tuesday, and Nancy wore the prettiest pink dress you ever did see. I was there, you know. Oh, my, yes. They said there couldn't be a weddin' of a Bishop boy without Granny Bee attendin'.

"Nancy's mama came from Florida with that Fred fella. Nancy asked Ruth Shatner quietlike if Ruth was goin' to marry Fred.

"You know what Nancy's mama said? Oh, mercy, Nancy was shocked down to her little toes. Ruth said she figured she'd just stay put in her house and Fred should stay put in his, and they'd see each other when the mood struck. She needed, Ruth told Nancy, her freedom to do as she liked. Now isn't that somethin'?

"Anyway, it was a lovely weddin' with a dancin' band playin' at the reception and all. Jana-John and Abe danced and

danced, gazin' at each other like two young people just meet-
in' and fallin' in love.

"Blue and Bram told me they surely did wish they were
the ones gettin' married. I said it would happen for 'em when
the time was right.

"Little did I know that Blue...

"Well, that's another whole story your Granny Bee will be
tellin' you the next time you come to call."

*   *   *   *   *

Don't miss TEXAS DAWN, *Blue's romance,*
coming your way in Silhouette Special Edition during
the summer of 1997!

Silhouette's newest series
YOURS TRULY

Love when you least expect it.

Where the written word plays a vital role in uniting couples—you're guaranteed a fun and exciting read every time!

Look for Marie Ferrarella's upcoming Yours Truly, *Traci on the Spot*, in March 1997.

Here's a special sneak preview....

1

Morgan Brigham slowly set down his coffee cup on the kitchen table and stared at the comic strip in the center of his paper. It was nestled in among approximately twenty others that were spread out across two pages. But this was the only one he made a point of reading faithfully each morning at breakfast.

This was the only one that mirrored *her* life.

He read each panel twice, as if he couldn't trust his own eyes. But he could. It was there, in black and white.

Morgan folded the paper slowly, thoughtfully, his mind not on his task. So Traci was getting engaged.

The realization gnawed at the lining of his stomach. He hadn't a clue as to why.

He had even less of a clue why he did what he did next.

Abandoning his coffee, now cool, and the newspaper, and ignoring the fact that this was going to make him late for the office, Morgan went to get a sheet of stationery from the den.

He didn't have much time.

Traci Richardson stared at the last frame she had just drawn. Debating, she glanced at the creature sprawled out on the kitchen floor.

"What do you think, Jeremiah? Too blunt?"

The dog, part bloodhound, part mutt, idly looked up from his rawhide bone at the sound of his name. Jeremiah gave her a look she felt free to interpret as ambivalent.

"Fine help you are. What if Daniel actually reads this and puts two and two together?"

Not that there was all that much chance that the man who had proposed to her, the very prosperous and busy Dr. Daniel Thane, would actually see the comic strip she drew for a living. Not unless the strip was taped to a bicuspid he was examining. Lately Daniel had gotten so busy he'd stopped reading anything but the morning headlines of the *Times*.

Still, you never knew. "I don't want to hurt his feelings," Traci continued, using Jeremiah as a sounding board. "It's just that Traci is overwhelmed by Donald's proposal and, see, she thinks the ring is going to swallow her up." To prove her point, Traci held up the drawing for the dog to view.

This time, he didn't even bother to lift his head.

Traci stared moodily at the small velvet box on the kitchen counter. It had sat there since Daniel had asked her to marry him last Sunday. Even if Daniel never read her comic strip, he was going to suspect something eventually. The very fact that she hadn't grabbed the ring from his hand and slid it onto her finger should have told him that she had doubts about their union.

Traci sighed. Daniel was a catch by any definition. So what was her problem? She kept waiting to be struck by that sunny ray of happiness. Daniel said he wanted to take care of her, to fulfill her every wish. And he was even willing to let her think about it before she gave him her answer.

Guilt nibbled at her. She should be dancing up and down, not wavering like a weather vane in a gale.

Pronouncing the strip completed, she scribbled her signature in the corner of the last frame and then sighed. Another week's work put to bed. She glanced at the pile of mail on the counter. She'd been bringing it in steadily from the mailbox since Monday, but the stack had gotten no farther than her kitchen. Sorting letters seemed the least heinous of all the annoying chores that faced her.

Traci paused as she noted a long envelope. Morgan Brigham. Why would Morgan be writing to her?

Curious, she tore open the envelope and quickly scanned the short note inside.

Dear Traci,

I'm putting the summerhouse up for sale. Thought you might want to come up and see it one more time before it goes up on the block. Or make a bid for it yourself. If memory serves, you once said you wanted to buy it. Either way, let me know. My number's on the card.

Take care,
Morgan

P.S. Got a kick out of *Traci on the Spot* this week.

Traci folded the letter. He read her strip. She hadn't known that. A feeling of pride silently coaxed a smile to her lips. After a beat, though, the rest of his note seeped into her consciousness. He was selling the house.

The summerhouse. A faded white building with brick trim. Suddenly, memories flooded her mind. Long, lazy afternoons that felt as if they would never end.

Morgan.

She looked at the far wall in the family room. There was a large framed photograph of her and Morgan standing before the summerhouse. Traci and Morgan. Morgan and Traci. Back then, it seemed their lives had been permanently intertwined. A bittersweet feeling of loss passed over her.

Traci quickly pulled the telephone over to her on the counter and tapped out the number on the keypad.

* * * * *

Look for TRACI ON THE SPOT
by Marie Ferrarella, coming to
Silhouette YOURS TRULY
in March 1997.

MILLION DOLLAR SWEEPSTAKES
OFFICIAL RULES
NO PURCHASE NECESSARY TO ENTER

1. To enter, follow the directions published. Method of entry may vary. For eligibility, entries must be received no later than March 31, 1998. No liability is assumed for printing errors, lost, late, non-delivered or misdirected entries.

    To determine winners, the sweepstakes numbers assigned to submitted entries will be compared against a list of randomly, preselected prize winning numbers. In the event all prizes are not claimed via the return of prize winning numbers, random drawings will be held from among all other entries received to award unclaimed prizes.

2. Prize winners will be determined no later than June 30, 1998. Selection of winning numbers and random drawings are under the supervision of D. L. Blair, Inc., an independent judging organization whose decisions are final. Limit: one prize to a family or organization. No substitution will be made for any prize, except as offered. Taxes and duties on all prizes are the sole responsibility of winners. Winners will be notified by mail. Odds of winning are determined by the number of eligible entries distributed and received.

3. Sweepstakes open to residents of the U.S. (except Puerto Rico), Canada and Europe who are 18 years of age or older, except employees and immediate family members of Torstar Corp., D. L. Blair, Inc., their affiliates, subsidiaries, and all other agencies, entities, and persons connected with the use, marketing or conduct of this sweepstakes. All applicable laws and regulations apply. Sweepstakes offer void wherever prohibited by law. Any litigation within the province of Quebec respecting the conduct and awarding of a prize in this sweepstakes must be submitted to the Régie des alcools, des courses et des jeux. In order to win a prize, residents of Canada will be required to correctly answer a time-limited arithmetical skill-testing question to be administered by mail.

4. Winners of major prizes (Grand through Fourth) will be obligated to sign and return an Affidavit of Eligibility and Release of Liability within 30 days of notification. In the event of non-compliance within this time period or if a prize is returned as undeliverable, D. L. Blair, Inc. may at its sole discretion, award that prize to an alternate winner. By acceptance of their prize, winners consent to use of their names, photographs or other likeness for purposes of advertising, trade and promotion on behalf of Torstar Corp., its affiliates and subsidiaries, without further compensation unless prohibited by law. Torstar Corp. and D. L. Blair, Inc., their affiliates and subsidiaries are not responsible for errors in printing of sweepstakes and prize winning numbers. In the event a duplication of a prize winning number occurs, a random drawing will be held from among all entries received with that prize winning number to award that prize.

5. This sweepstakes is presented by Torstar Corp., its subsidiaries and affiliates in conjunction with book, merchandise and/or product offerings. The number of prizes to be awarded and their value are as follows: Grand Prize — $1,000,000 (payable at $33,333.33 a year for 30 years); First Prize — $50,000; Second Prize — $10,000; Third Prize — $5,000; 3 Fourth Prizes — $1,000 each; 10 Fifth Prizes — $250 each; 1,000 Sixth Prizes — $10 each. Values of all prizes are in U.S. currency. Prizes in each level will be presented in different creative executions, including various currencies, vehicles, merchandise and travel. Any presentation of a prize level in a currency other than U.S. currency represents an approximate equivalent to the U.S. currency prize for that level, at that time. Prize winners will have the opportunity of selecting any prize offered for that level; however, the actual non U.S. currency equivalent prize if offered and selected, shall be awarded at the exchange rate existing at 3:00 P.M. New York time on March 31, 1998. A travel prize option, if offered and selected by winner, must be completed within 12 months of selection and is subject to: traveling companion(s) completing and returning of a Release of Liability prior to travel; and hotel and flight accommodations availability. For a current list of all prize options offered within prize levels, send a self-addressed, stamped envelope (WA residents need not affix postage) to: MILLION DOLLAR SWEEPSTAKES Prize Options, P.O. Box 4456, Blair, NE 68009-4456, USA.

6. For a list of prize winners (available after July 31, 1998) send a separate, stamped, self-addressed envelope to: MILLION DOLLAR SWEEPSTAKES Winners, P.O. Box 4459, Blair, NE 68009-4459, USA.

You know where the MEN are....

SILHOUETTE®

Desire®

MAN OF THE MONTH:
He's the sexiest hero around...

MOM7R

As seen on TV!
Free Gift Offer

With a Free Gift proof-of-purchase from any Silhouette® book,
you can receive a beautiful cubic zirconia pendant.

This gorgeous marquise-shaped stone is a genuine cubic
zirconia—accented by an 18" gold tone necklace.

(Approximate retail value $19.95)

Send for yours today...
compliments of 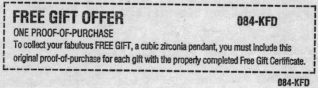 *Silhouette*®

To receive your free gift, a cubic zirconia pendant, send us one original proof-of-purchase, photocopies not accepted, from the back of any Silhouette Romance™, Silhouette Desire®, Silhouette Special Edition®, Silhouette Intimate Moments® or Silhouette Yours Truly™ title available in February, March and April at your favorite retail outlet, together with the Free Gift Certificate, plus a check or money order for $1.65 U.S./$2.15 CAN. (do not send cash) to cover postage and handling, payable to Silhouette Free Gift Offer. We will send you the specified gift. Allow 6 to 8 weeks for delivery. Offer good until April 30, 1997 or while quantities last. Offer valid in the U.S. and Canada only.

Free Gift Certificate

Name: _____

Address: _____

City: _____ State/Province: _____ Zip/Postal Code: _____

Mail this certificate, one proof-of-purchase and a check or money order for postage and handling to: SILHOUETTE FREE GIFT OFFER 1997. In the U.S.: 3010 Walden Avenue, P.O. Box 9077, Buffalo NY 14269-9077. In Canada: P.O. Box 613, Fort Erie, Ontario L2Z 5X3.

FREE GIFT OFFER
ONE PROOF-OF-PURCHASE

084-KFD

To collect your fabulous FREE GIFT, a cubic zirconia pendant, you must include this original proof-of-purchase for each gift with the properly completed Free Gift Certificate.

084-KFD

You're About to Become a *Privileged Woman*

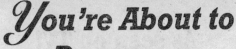

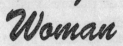

Reap the rewards of fabulous free gifts and
benefits with proofs-of-purchase from
Silhouette and Harlequin books

Pages & Privileges™

It's our way of thanking you for
buying our books at your
favorite retail stores.

PROOF OF PURCHASE
SD-PP22
Offer expires March 31, 1997

**Harlequin and Silhouette—
the most privileged readers in the world!**

For more information about Harlequin and
Silhouette's PAGES & PRIVILEGES program call the
Pages & Privileges Benefits Desk: 1-503-794-2499

Silhouette®

SD-PP22